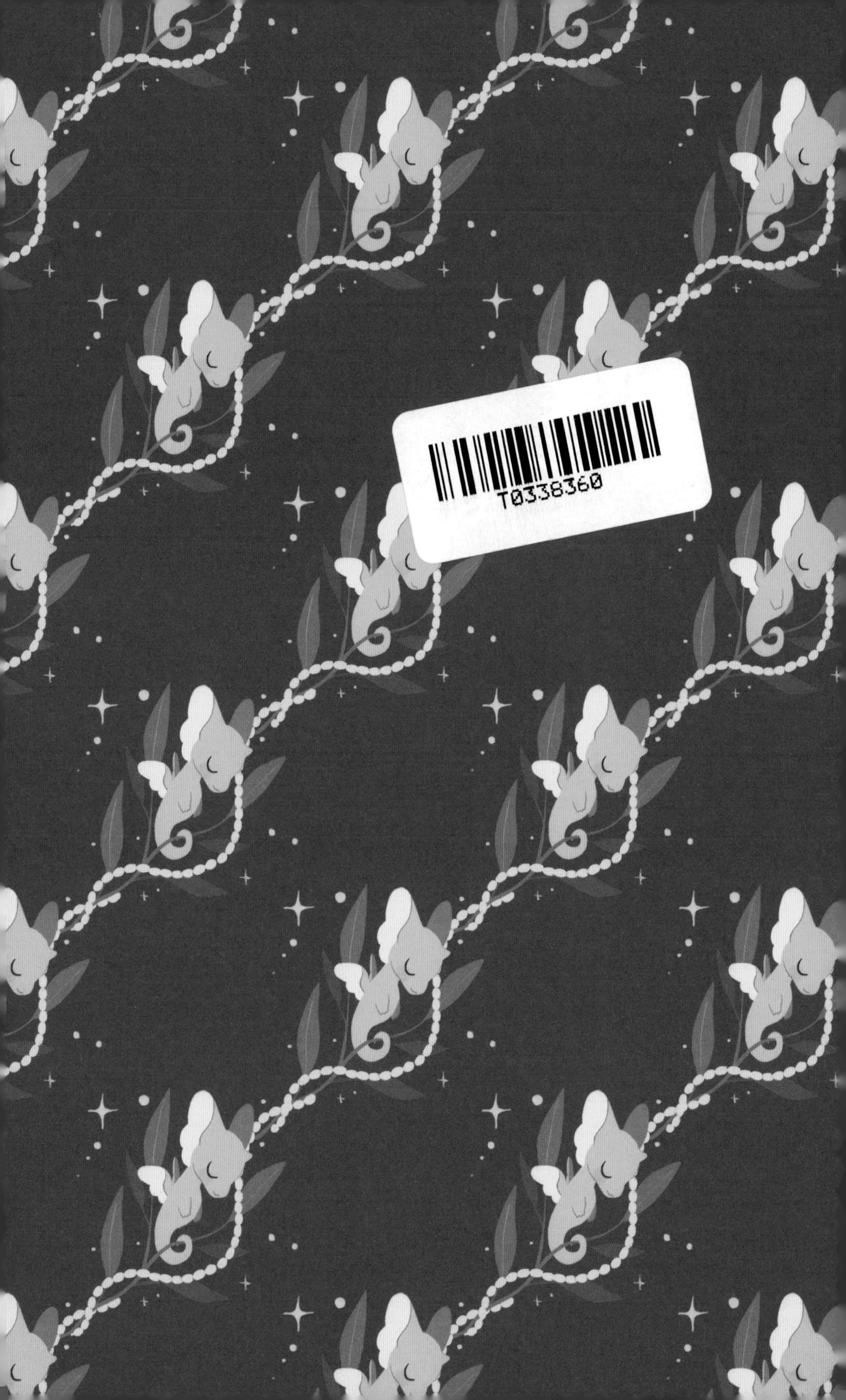

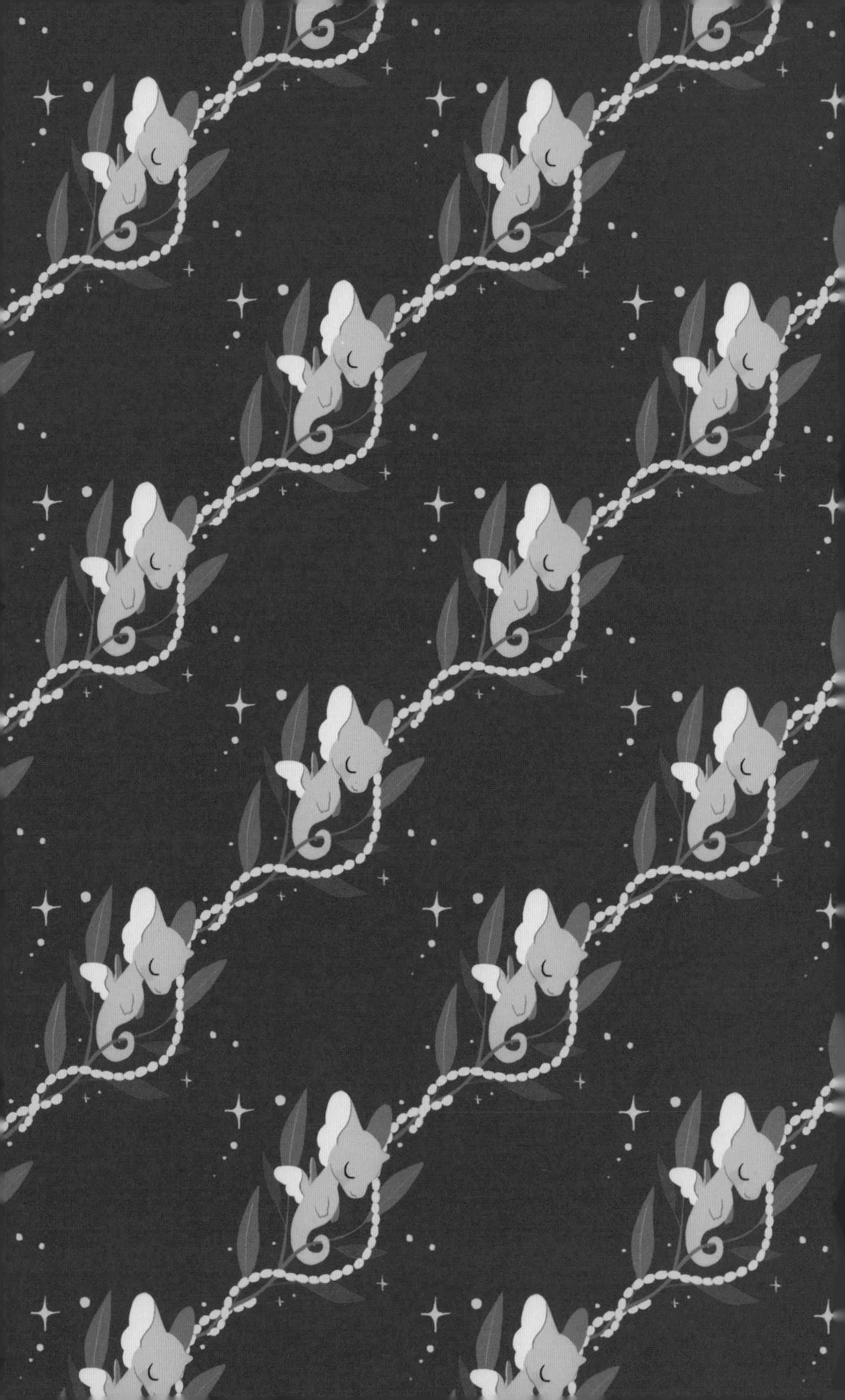

# AQUICORN
# COVE

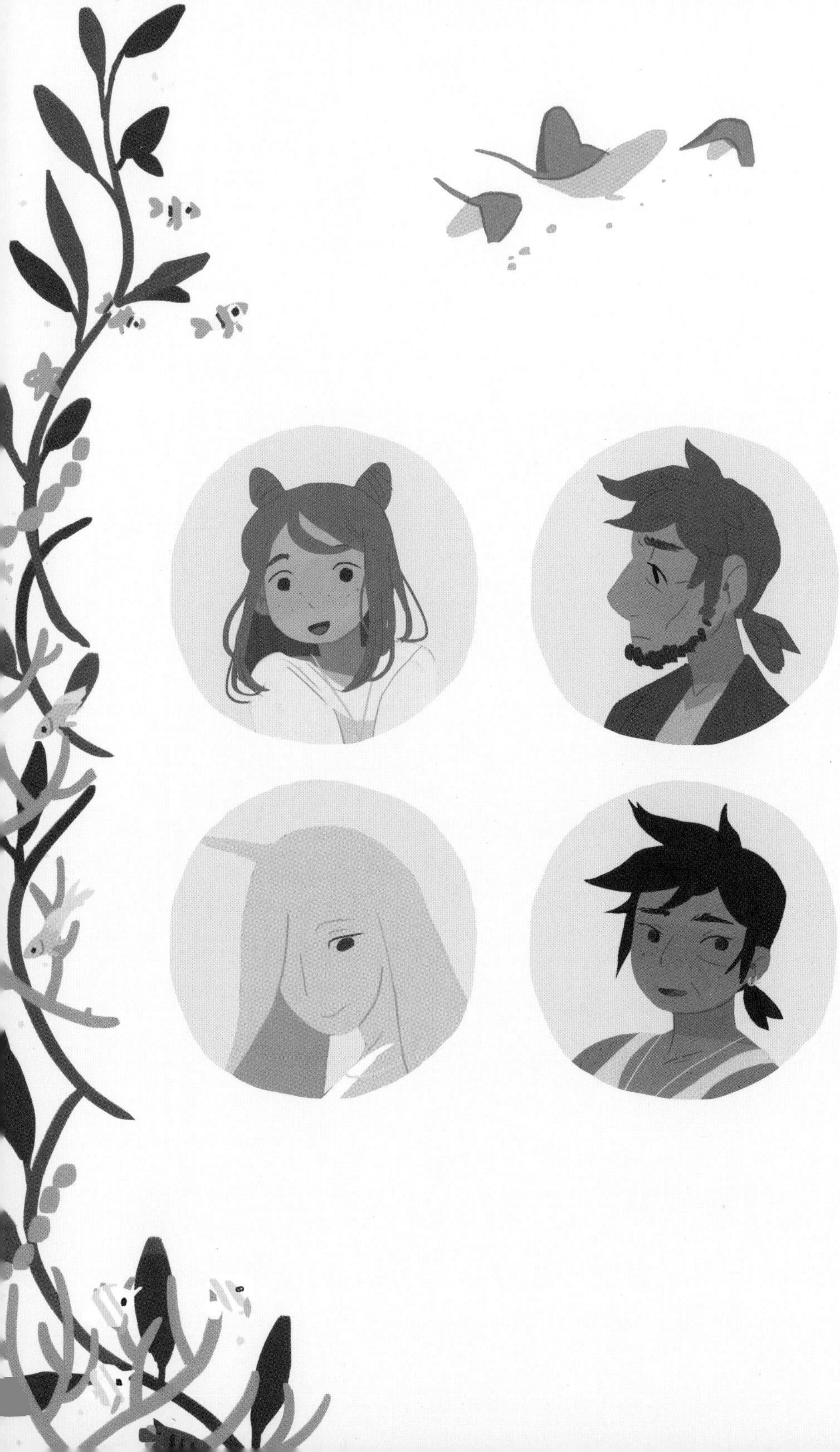

# AQUICORN COVE

WRITTEN & ILLUSTRATED BY

**Katie O'Neill**

LETTERED BY
Crank!

DESIGNED BY
Hilary Thompson

EDITED BY
Ari Yarwood

ONI PRESS

AN ONI PRESS PUBLICATION

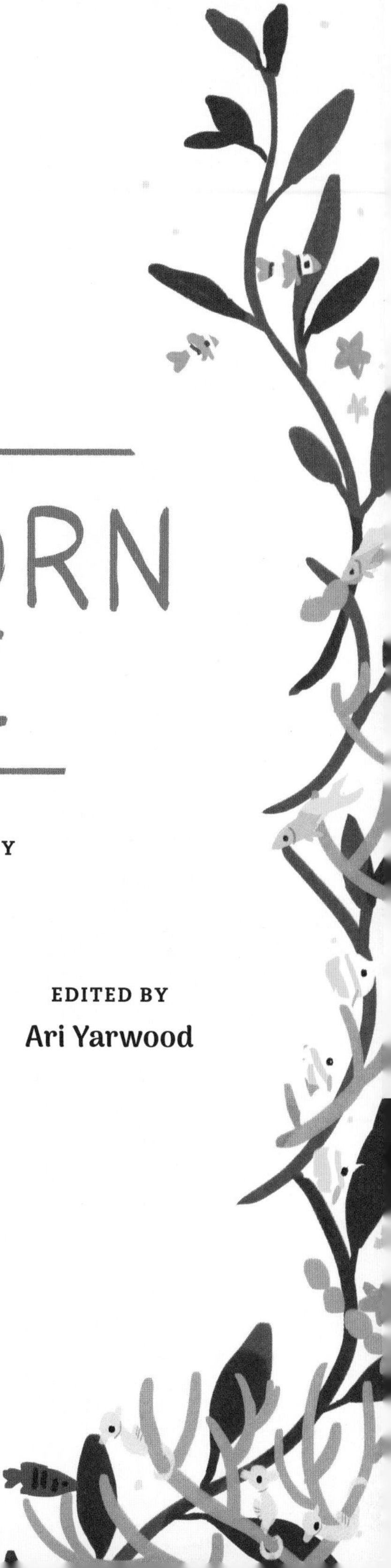

**PUBLISHED BY ONI PRESS, INC.**

Joe Nozemack, *founder & chief financial officer*
James Lucas Jones, *publisher*
Charlie Chu, *v.p. of creative & business development*
Brad Rooks, *director of operations*
Melissa Meszaros, *director of publicity*
Margot Wood, *director of sales*
Sandy Tanaka, *marketing design manager*
Amber O'Neill, *special projects manager*
Troy Look, *director of design & production*
Hilary Thompson, *senior graphic designer*
Kate Z. Stone, *graphic designer*
Sonja Synak, *junior graphic designer*
Angie Knowles, *digital prepress lead*
Ari Yarwood, *executive editor*
Sarah Gaydos, *editorial director of licensed publishing*
Robin Herrera, *senior editor*
Desiree Wilson, *associate editor*
Alissa Sallah, *administrative assistant*
Jung Lee, *logistics associate*
Scott Sharkey, *warehouse assistant*

onipress.com • facebook.com/onipress
twitter.com/onipress • onipress.tumblr.com
instagram.com/onipress

@strangelykatie • ktoneill.com

First Edition: October 2018
ISBN: 978-1-62010-529-0
eISBN: 978-1-62010-530-6

1 2 3 4 5 6 7 8 9 10

Library of Congress Control Number: 2018940553

Printed in China.

This book is for everyone who protects the sea,
and for those who will inherit the responsibility.
Thank you for taking care of our beautiful world.

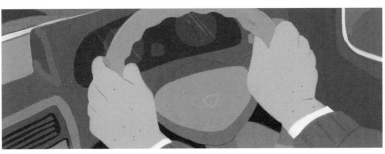

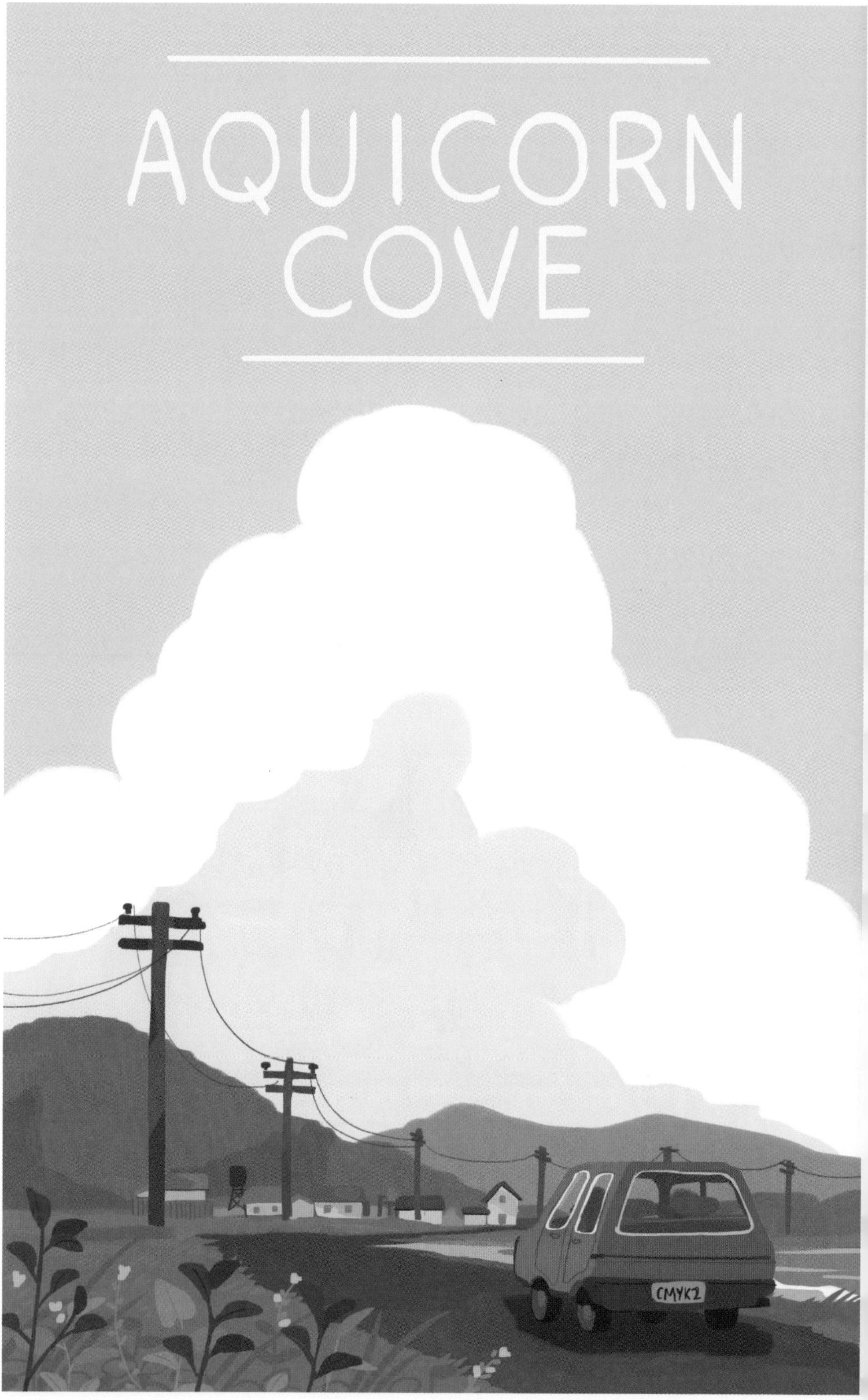
AQUICORN
COVE
CMYK2

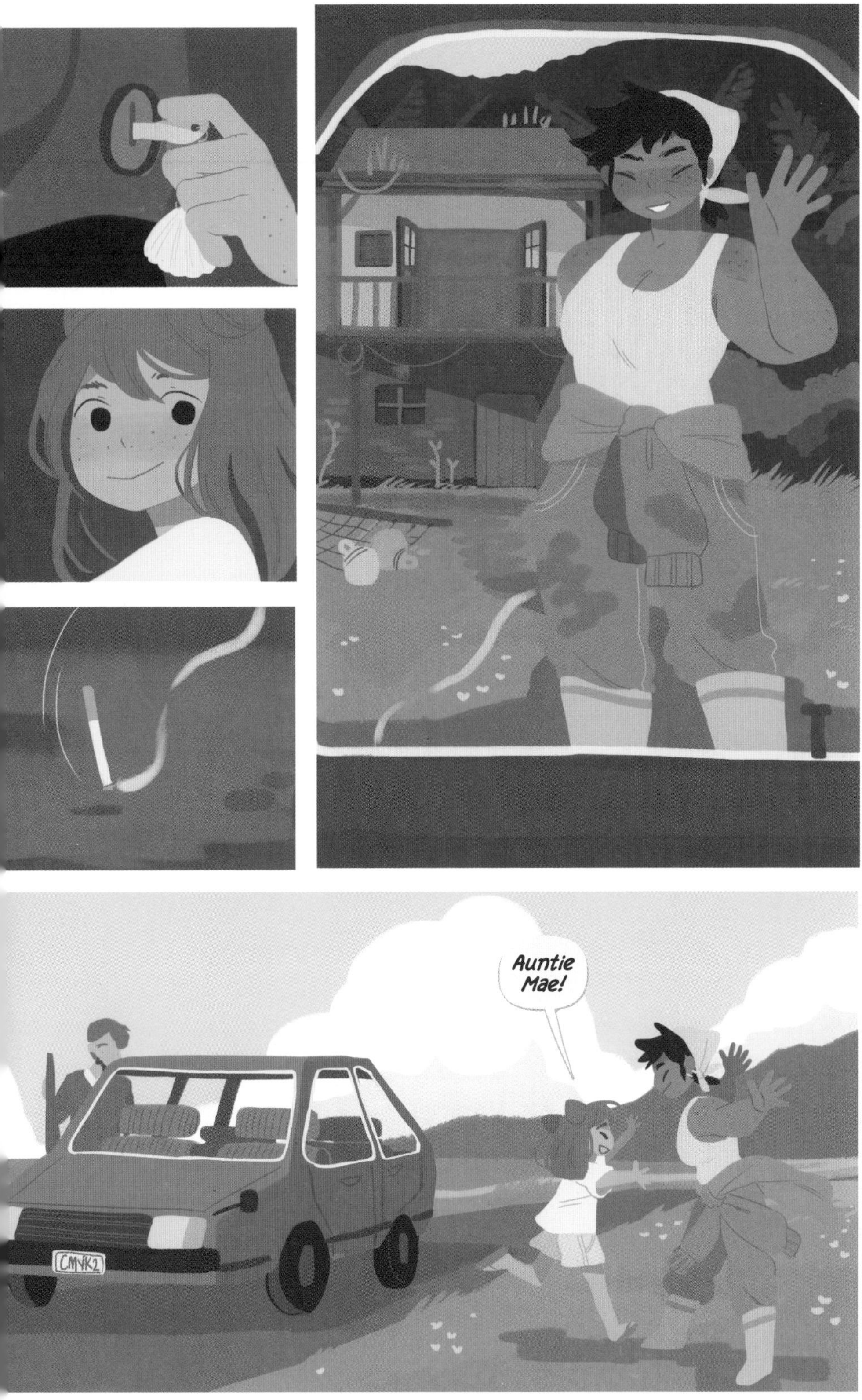
Auntie Mae!
CMYK2

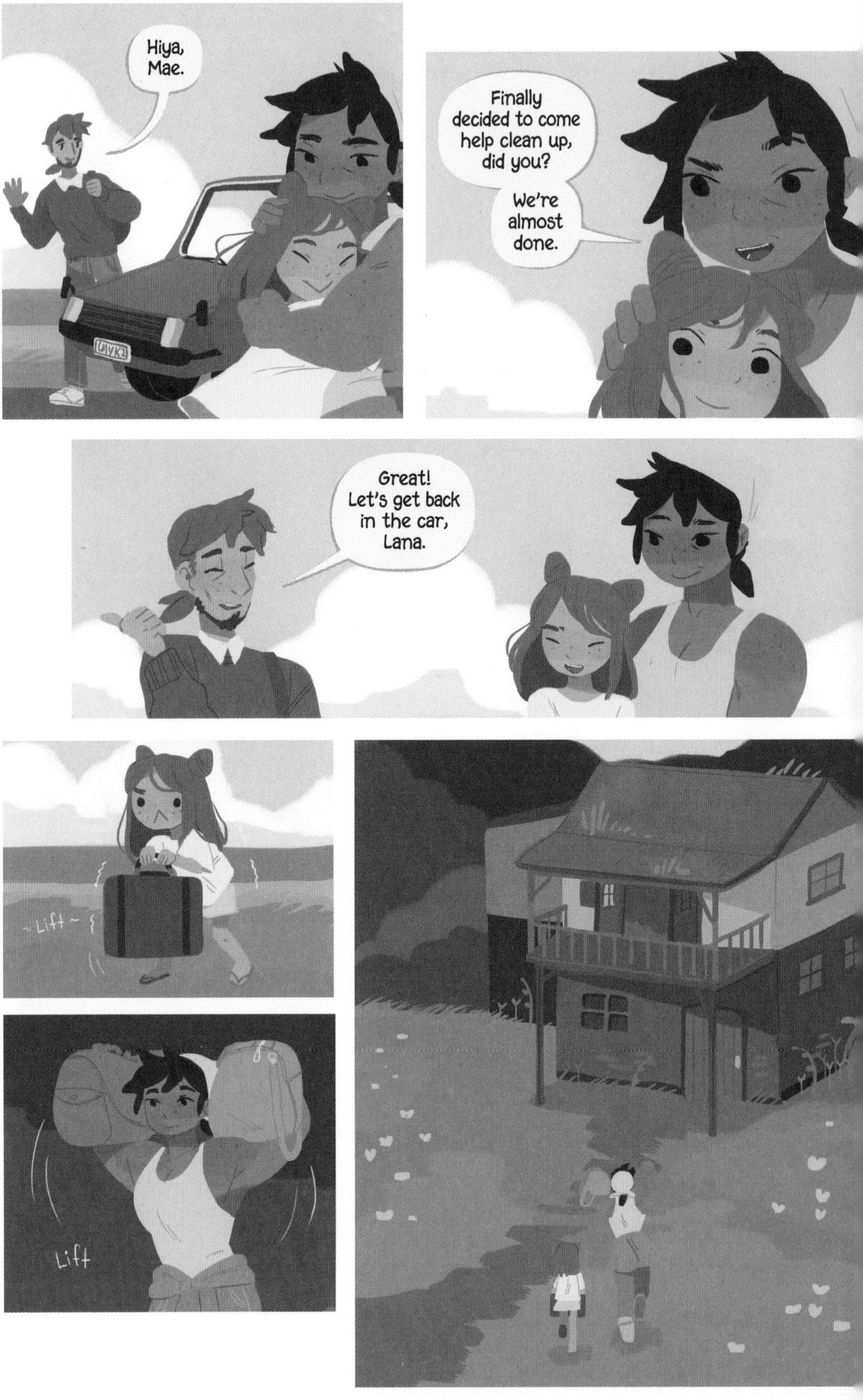
Hiya,
Mae.
Finally decided to come help clean up, did you?
We're almost done.
Great! Let's get back in the car, Lana.
~Lift~
Lift

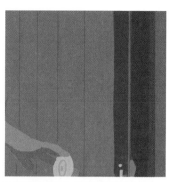

Geez, Mae.

You didn't tell me it stormed in here, too.

Haven't you ever heard of bohemian?

Melody was always the tidy one, huh?

Yeah.

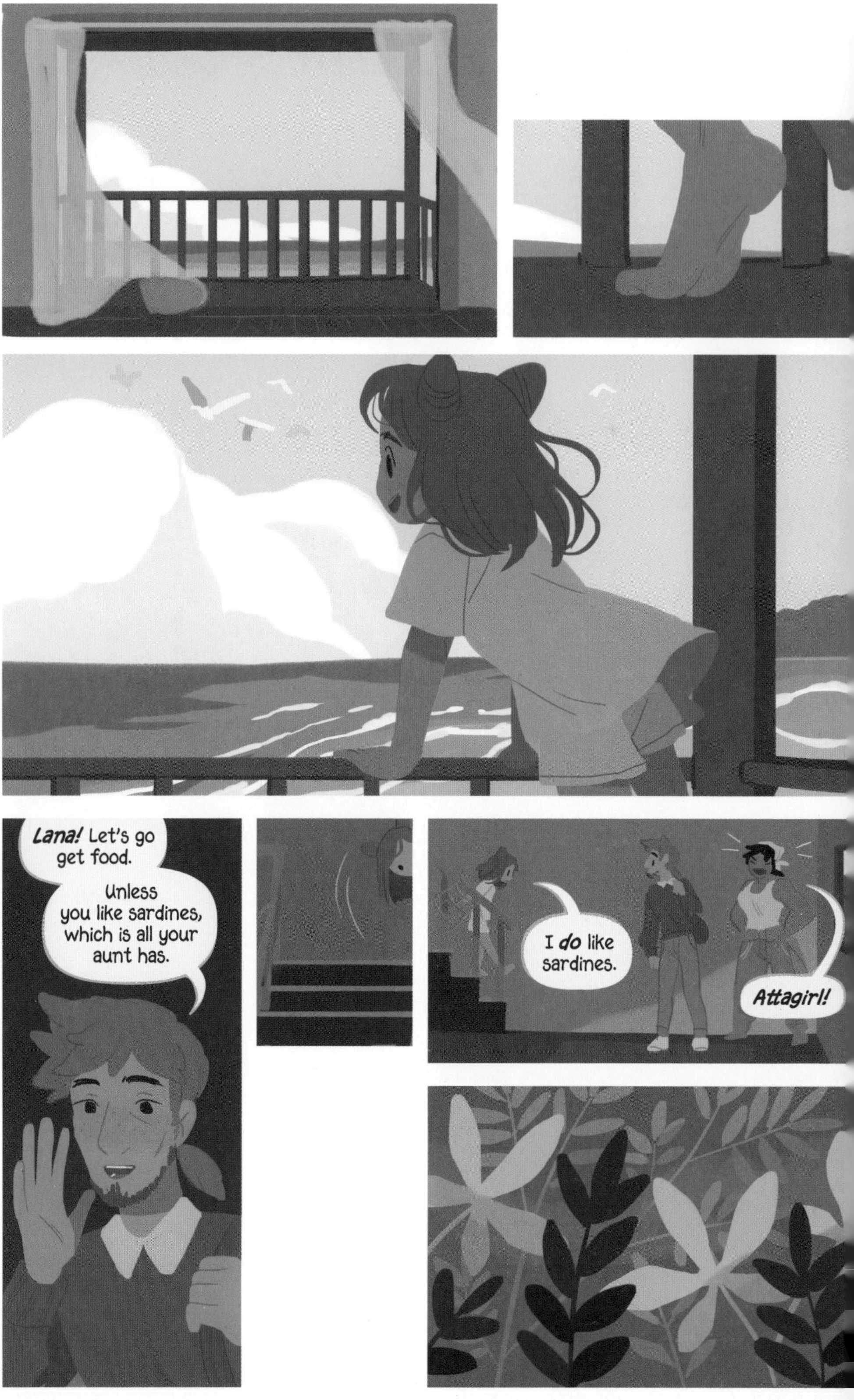

Lana! Let's go get food.
Unless you like sardines, which is all your aunt has.
I do like sardines.
Attagirl!

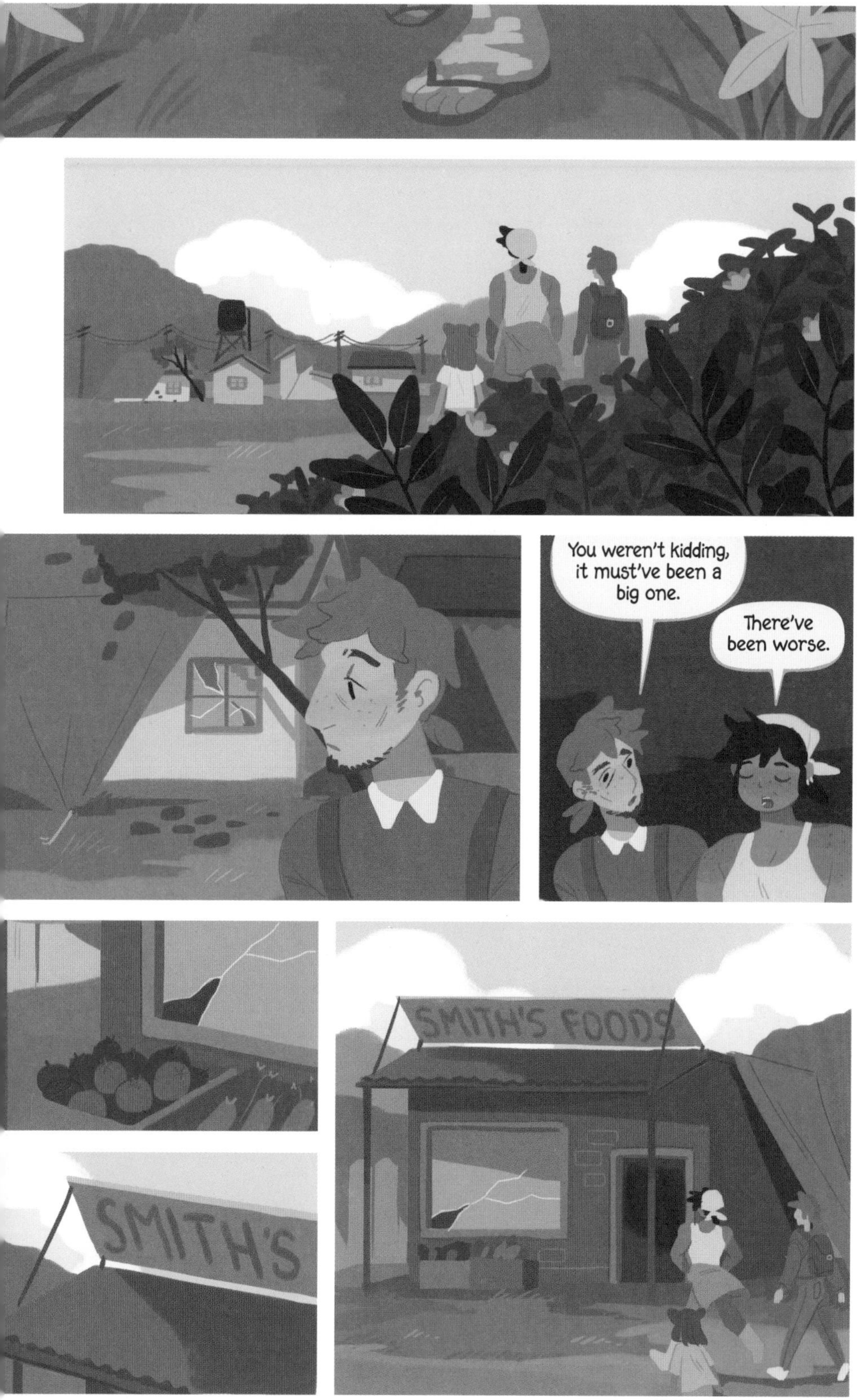
You weren't kidding, it must've been a big one.
There've been worse.
SMITH'S FOODS
SMITH'S

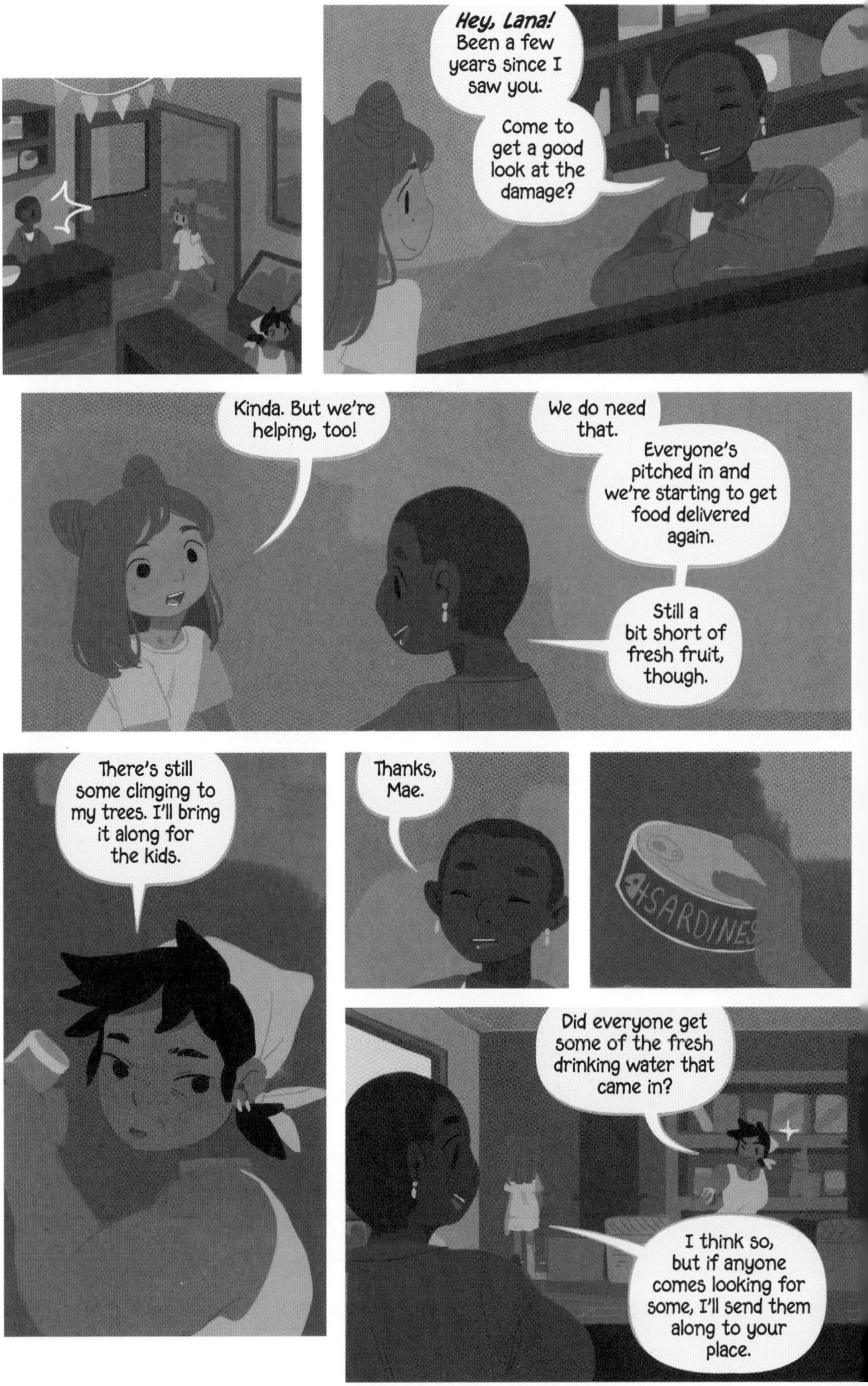

*Hey, Lana!* Been a few years since I saw you.
Come to get a good look at the damage?
Kinda. But we're helping, too!
We do need that.
Everyone's pitched in and we're starting to get food delivered again.
Still a bit short of fresh fruit, though.
There's still some clinging to my trees. I'll bring it along for the kids.
Thanks, Mae.
SARDINES
Did everyone get some of the fresh drinking water that came in?
I think so, but if anyone comes looking for some, I'll send them along to your place.

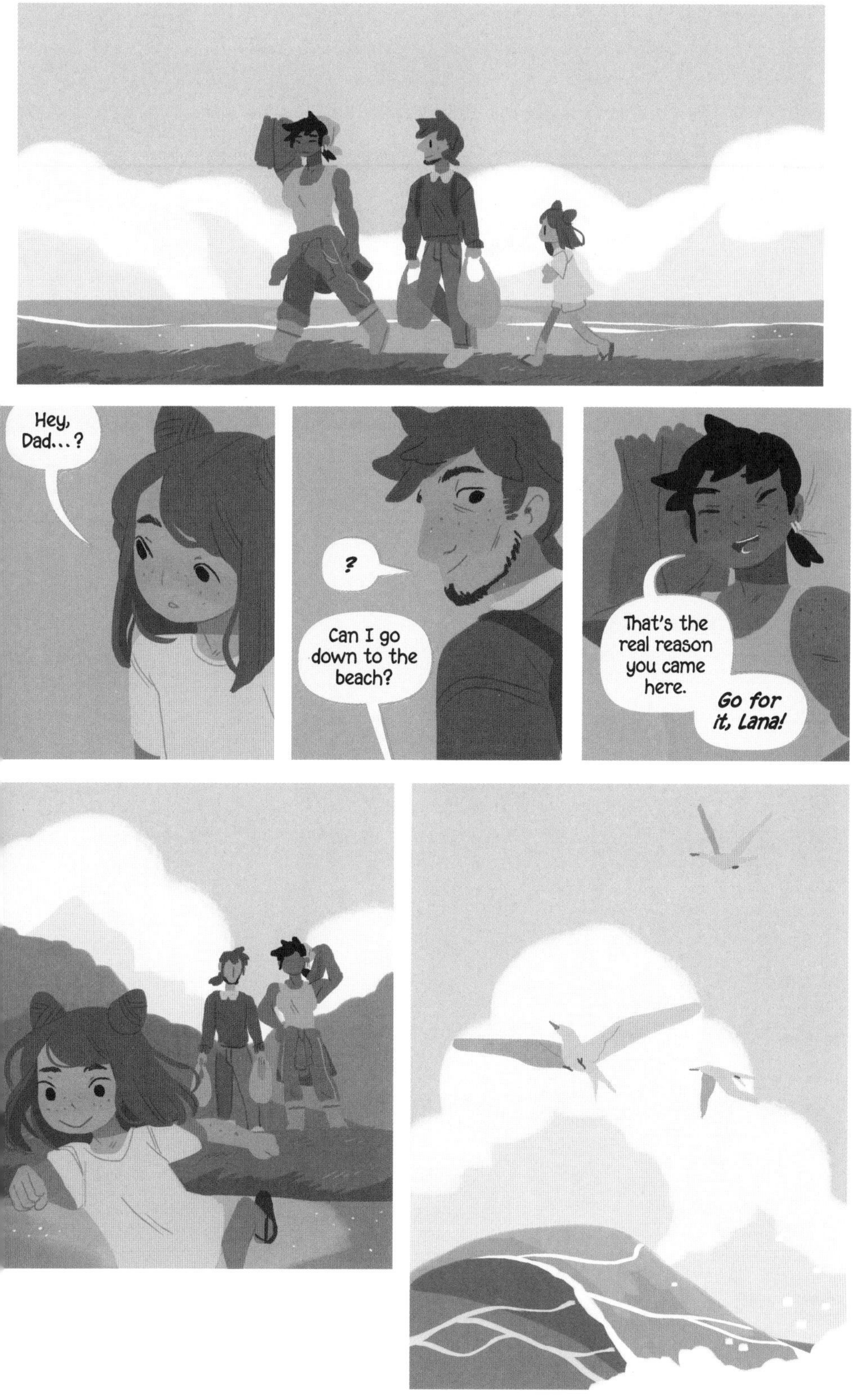
Hey, Dad...?
?
Can I go down to the beach?
That's the real reason you came here.
Go for it, Lana!

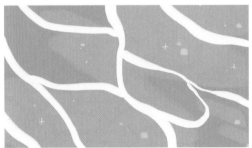

I came here so many times with my mom...

...she wanted to make sure I loved the sea.

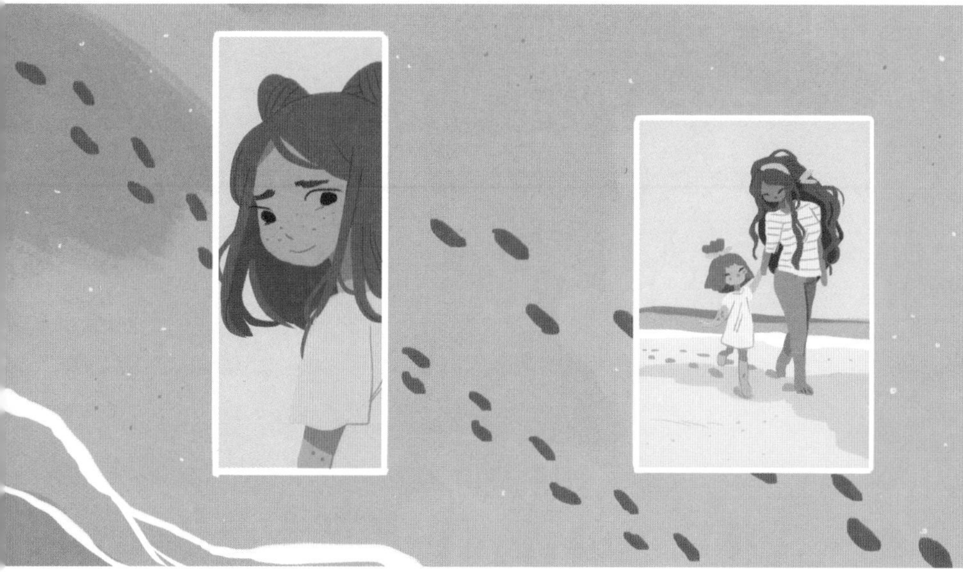

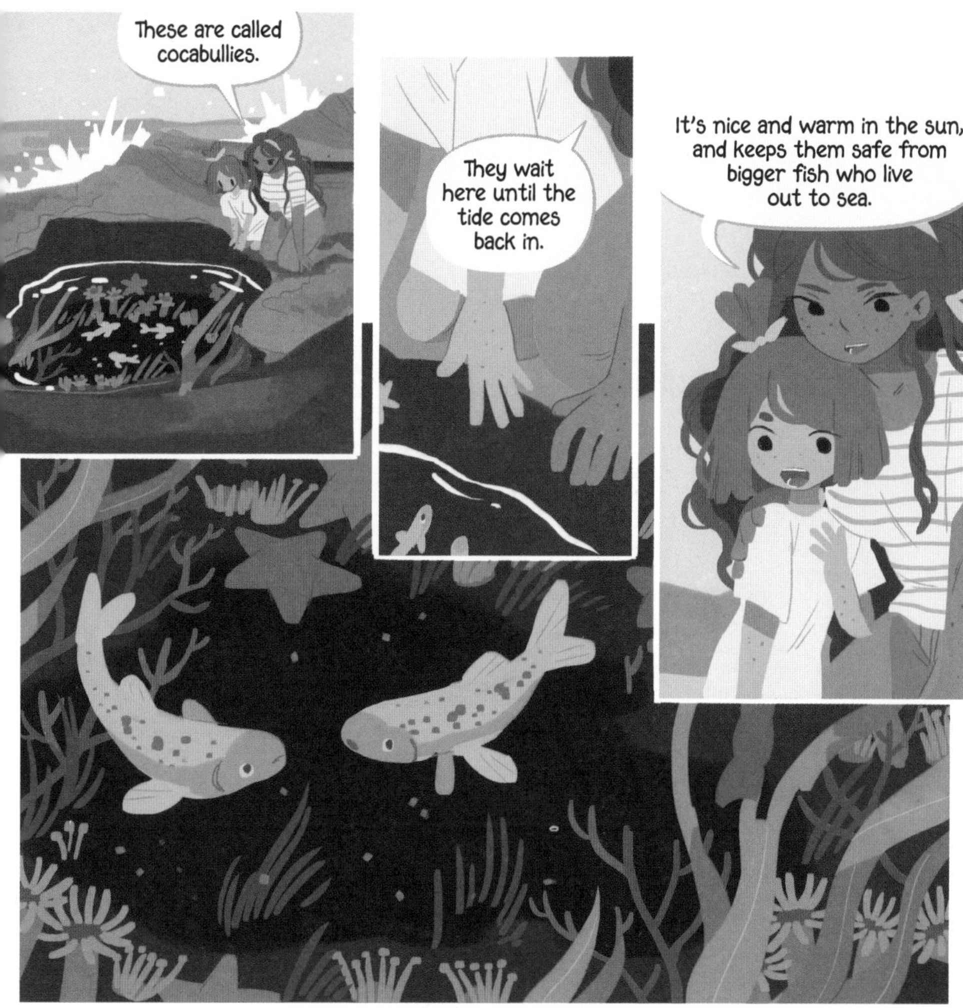
These are called cocabullies.
They wait here until the tide comes back in.
It's nice and warm in the sun, and keeps them safe from bigger fish who live out to sea.

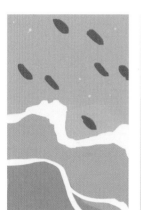

18

Stay right there! I'll come back and get you!

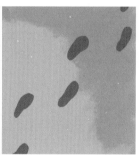

Do you know what it is, Auntie?

I knew the name once, but I've forgotten it now.

Near enough a seahorse, though.

How do I look after it?

Keep it in the water you found it in, and feed it brine shrimp.

That's what seahorses like to eat.

He'll be all right, don't you worry!

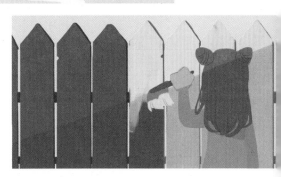

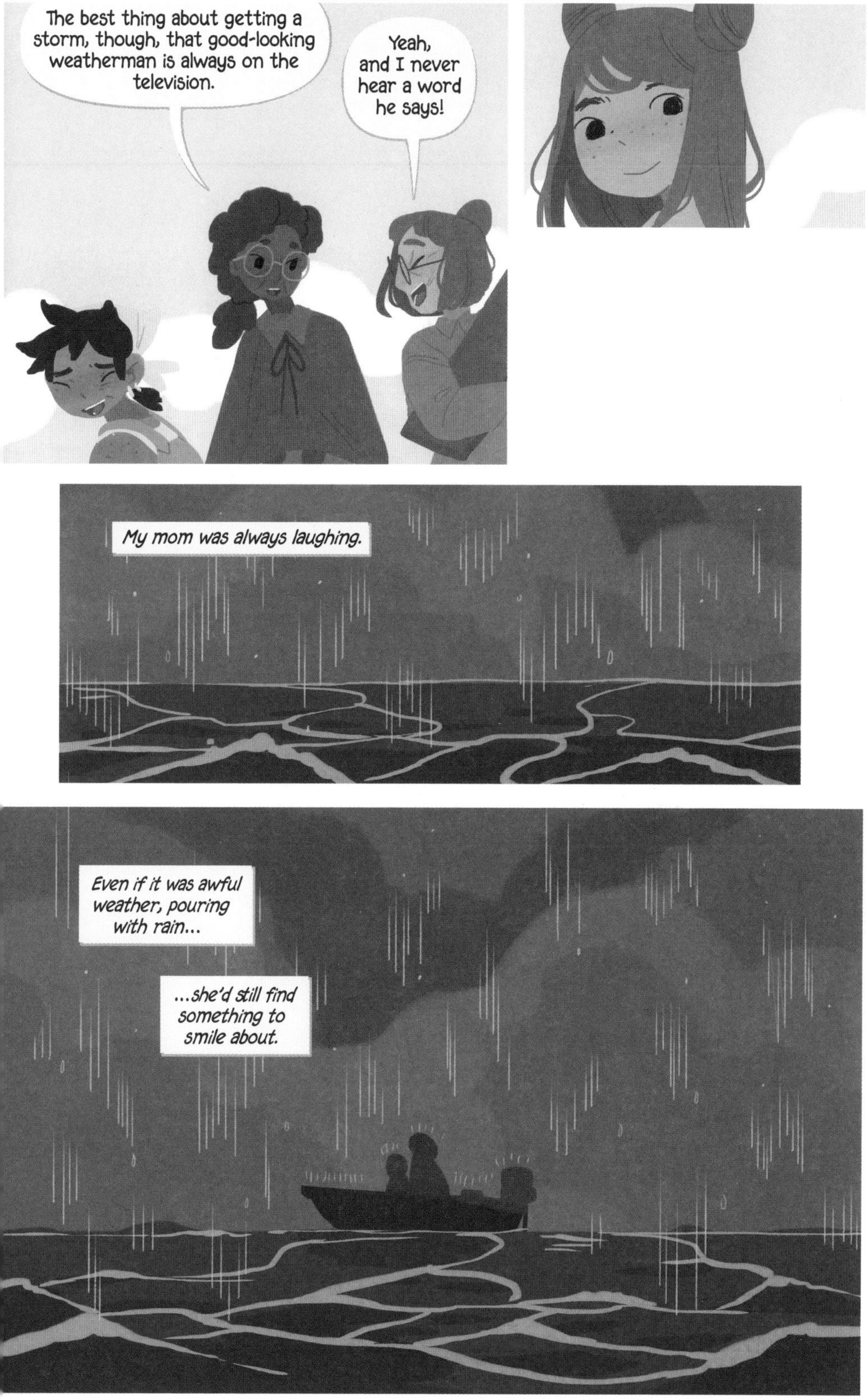
The best thing about getting a storm, though, that good-looking weatherman is always on the television.
Yeah, and I never hear a word he says!
My mom was always laughing.
Even if it was awful weather, pouring with rain...
...she'd still find something to smile about.

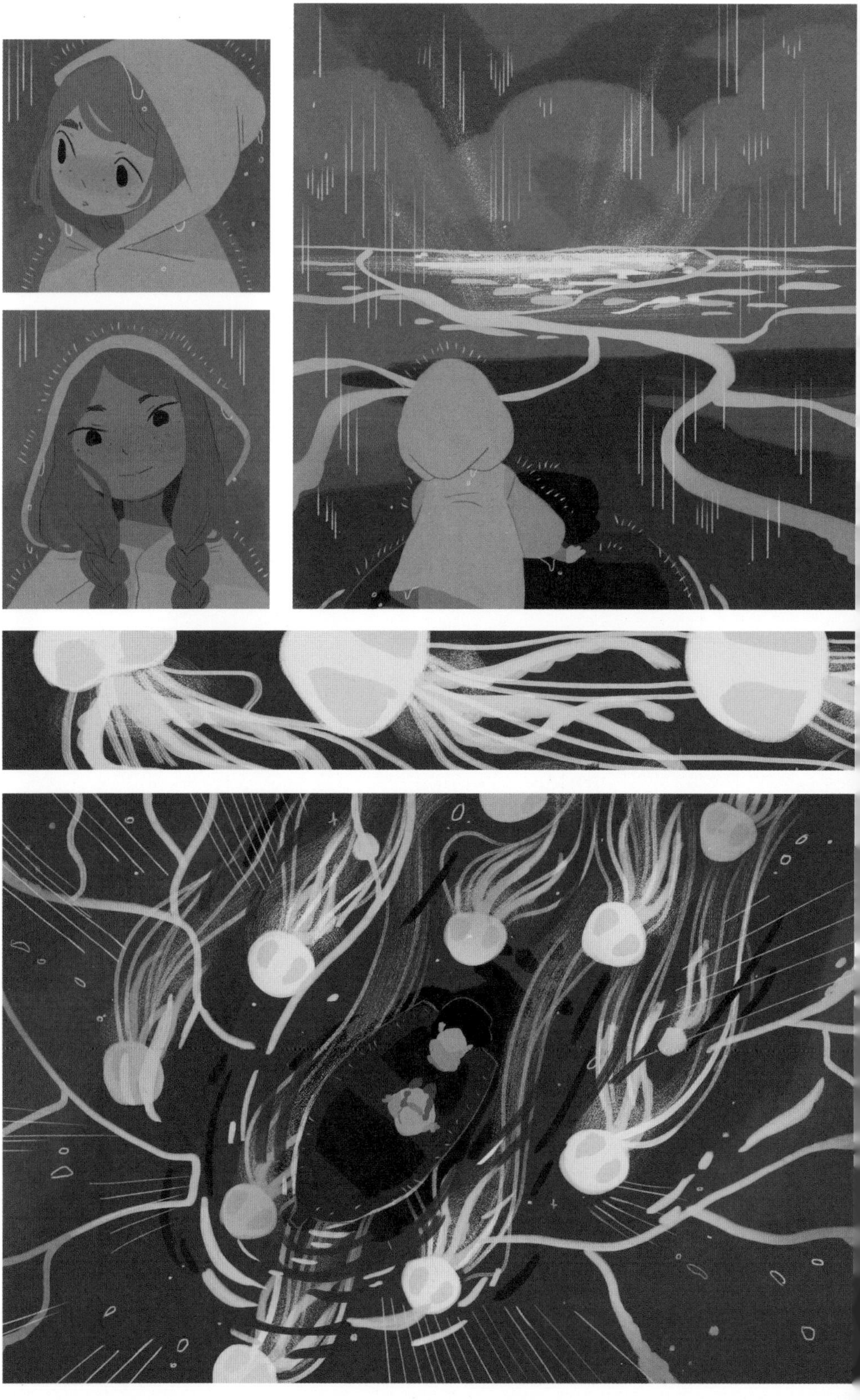

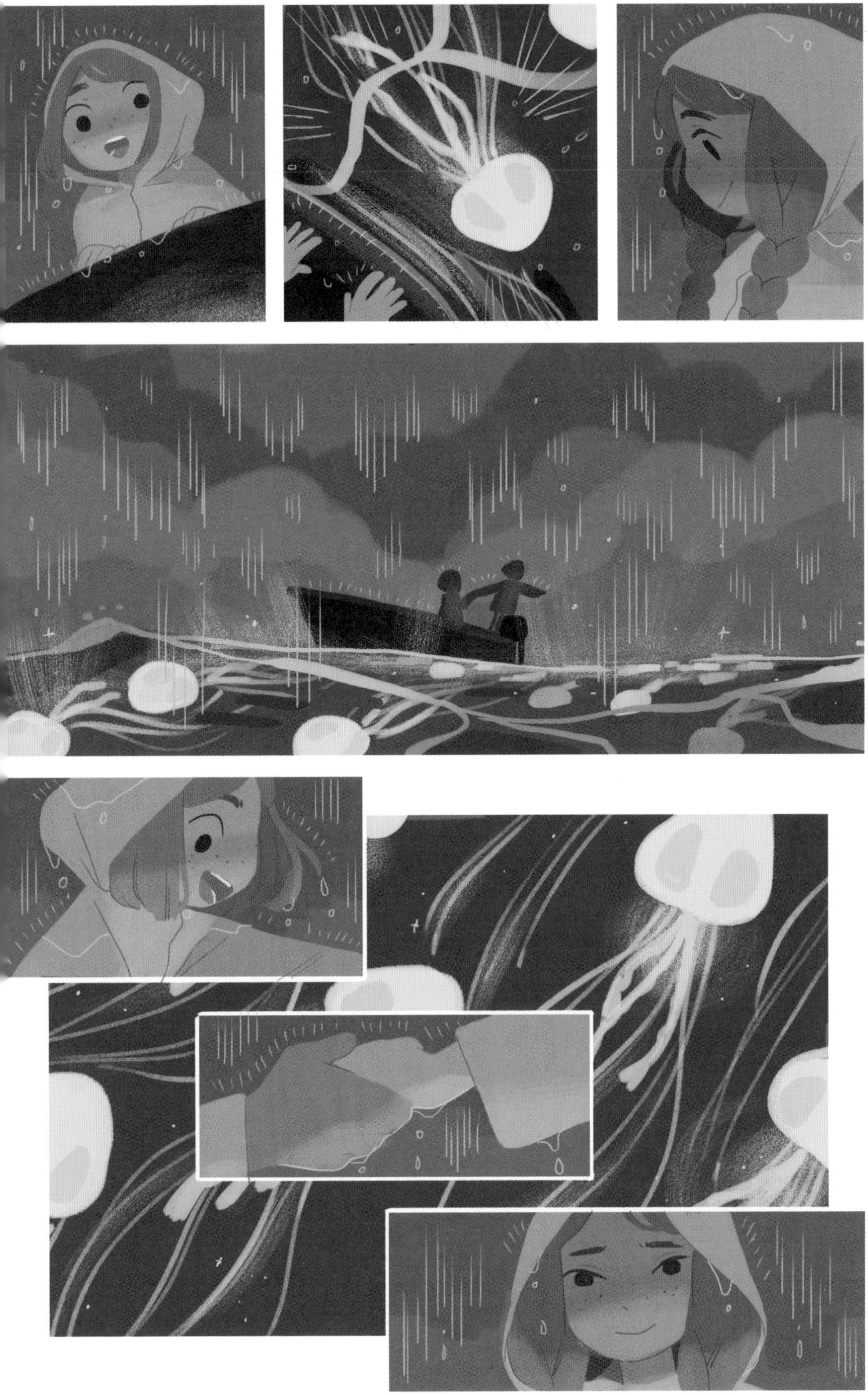

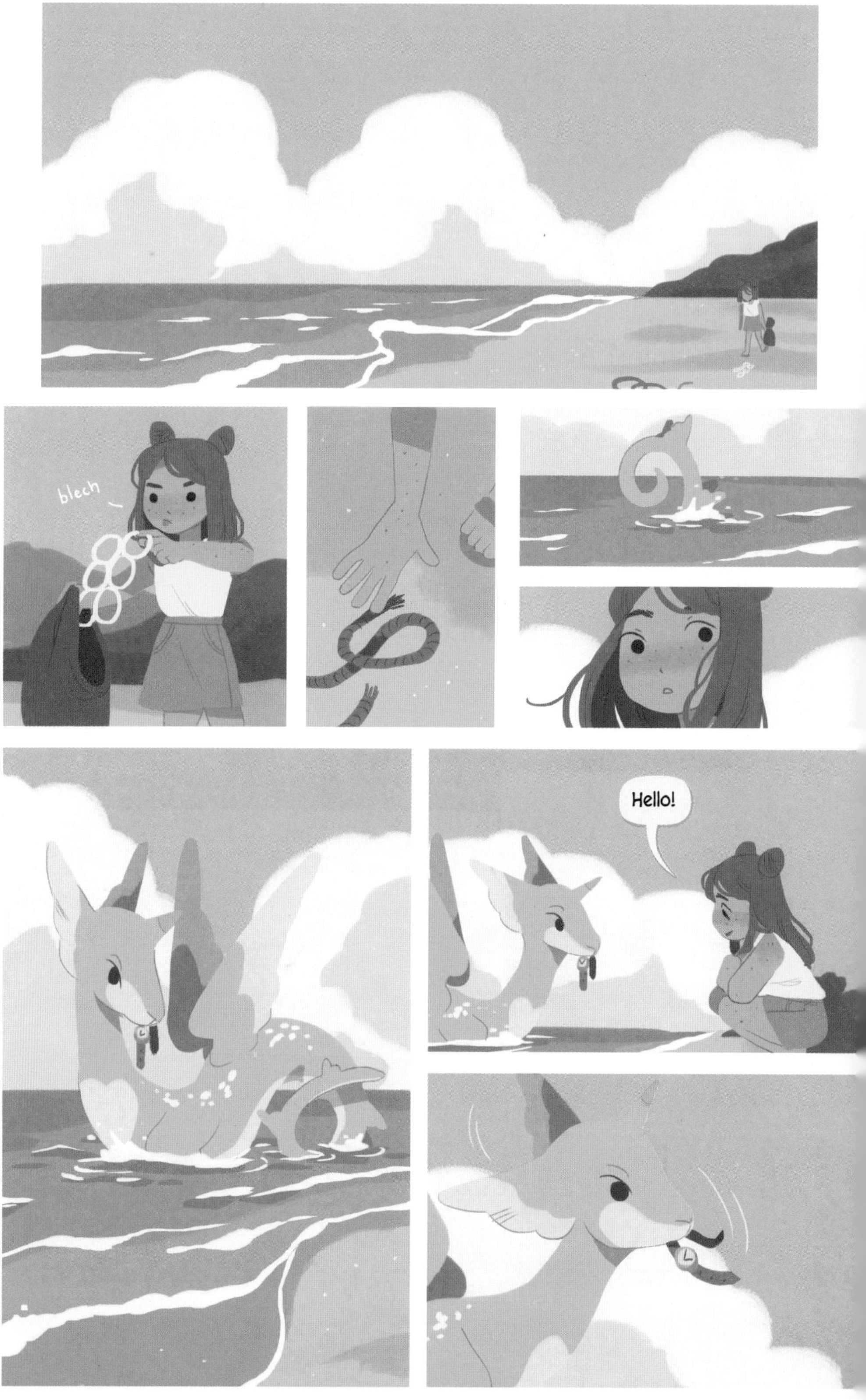
blech
Hello!

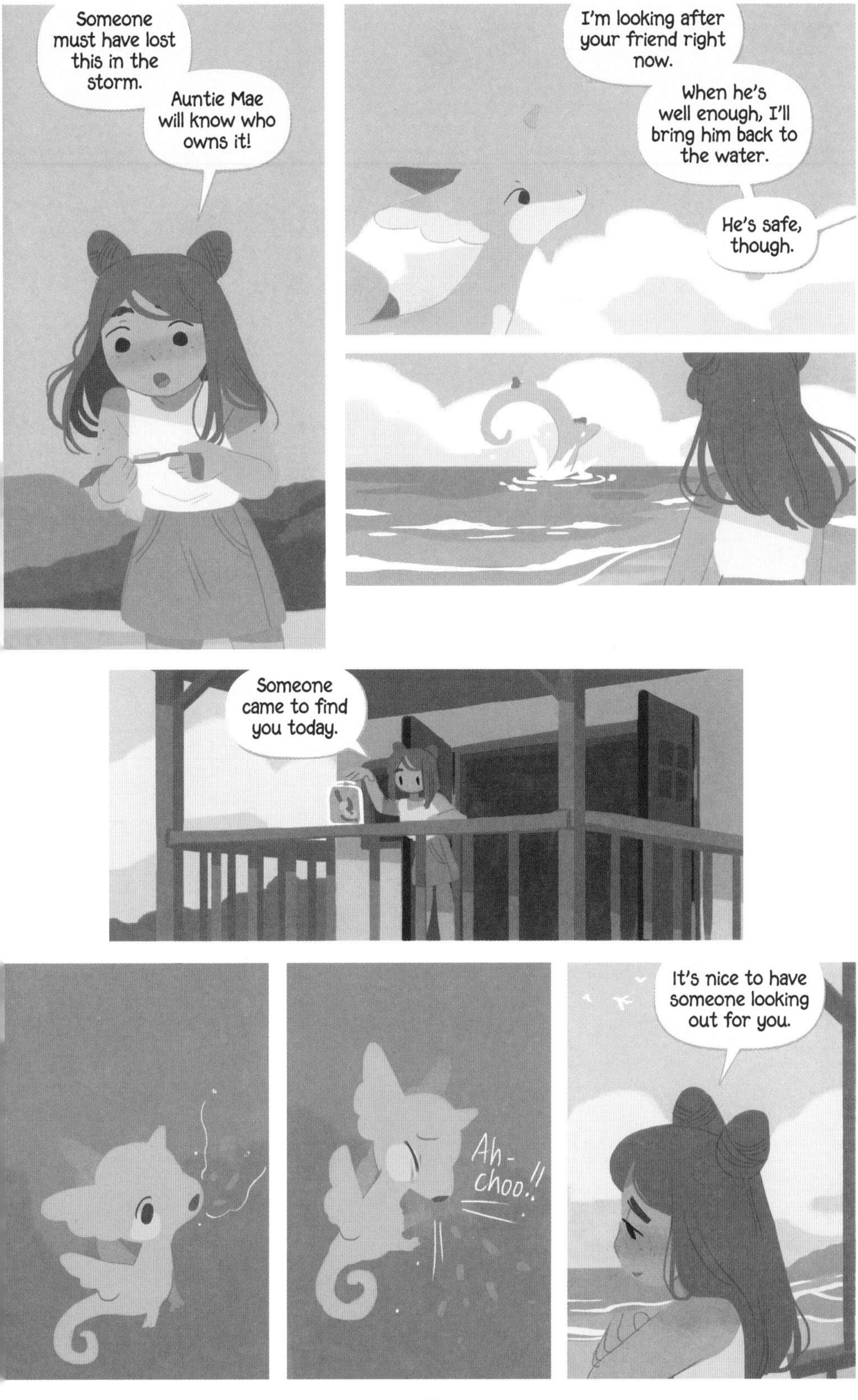
Someone must have lost this in the storm.
Auntie Mae will know who owns it!
I'm looking after your friend right now.
When he's well enough, I'll bring him back to the water.
He's safe, though.
Someone came to find you today.
Ah-choo!!
It's nice to have someone looking out for you.

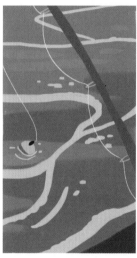

This is the perfect time to fish.

It's dinnertime for them too, so they're keen for an easy meal.

Ah!

Give it a snag to hook them, then gently reel it in.

26

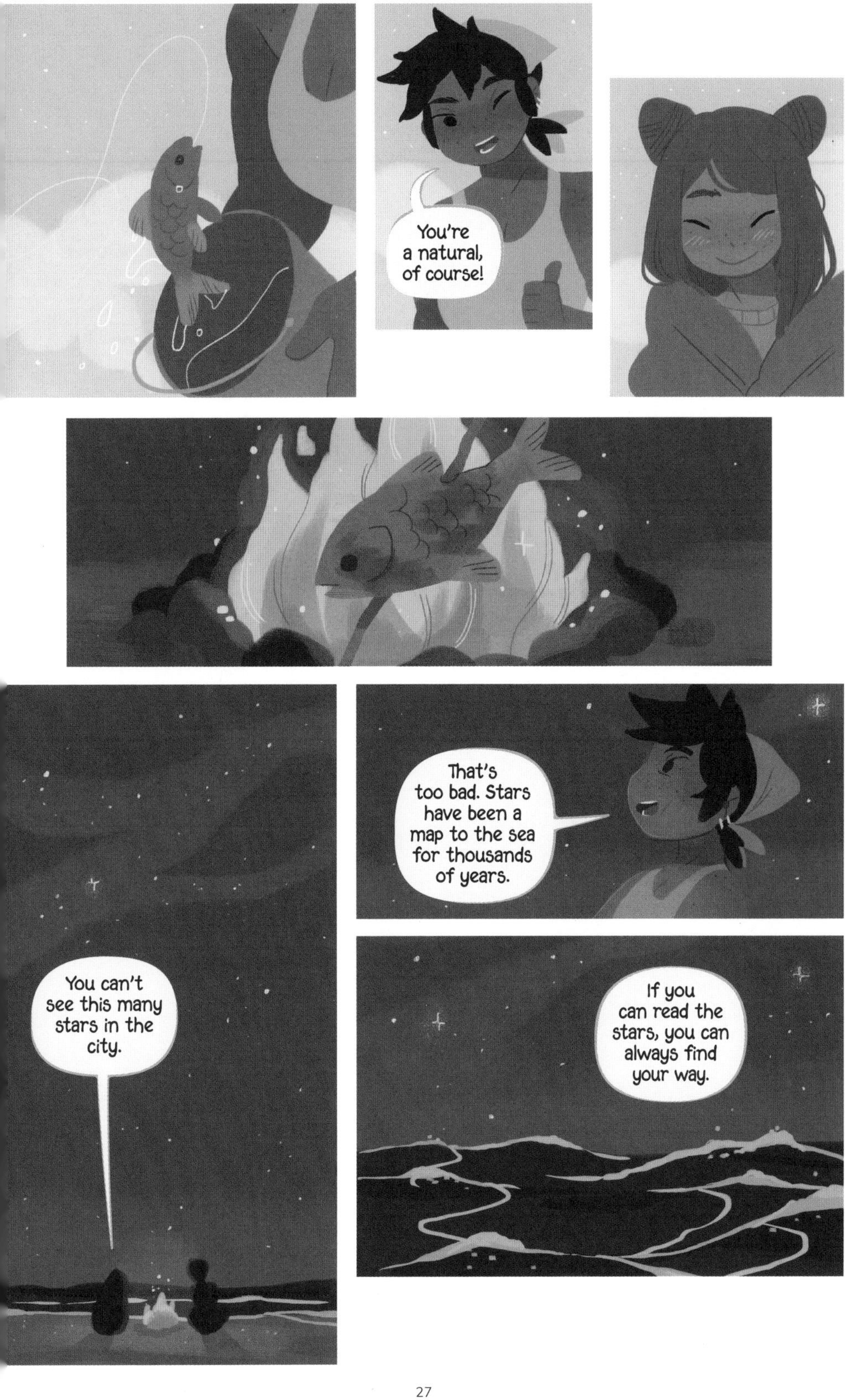
You're a natural, of course!
You can't see this many stars in the city.
That's too bad. Stars have been a map to the sea for thousands of years.
If you can read the stars, you can always find your way.

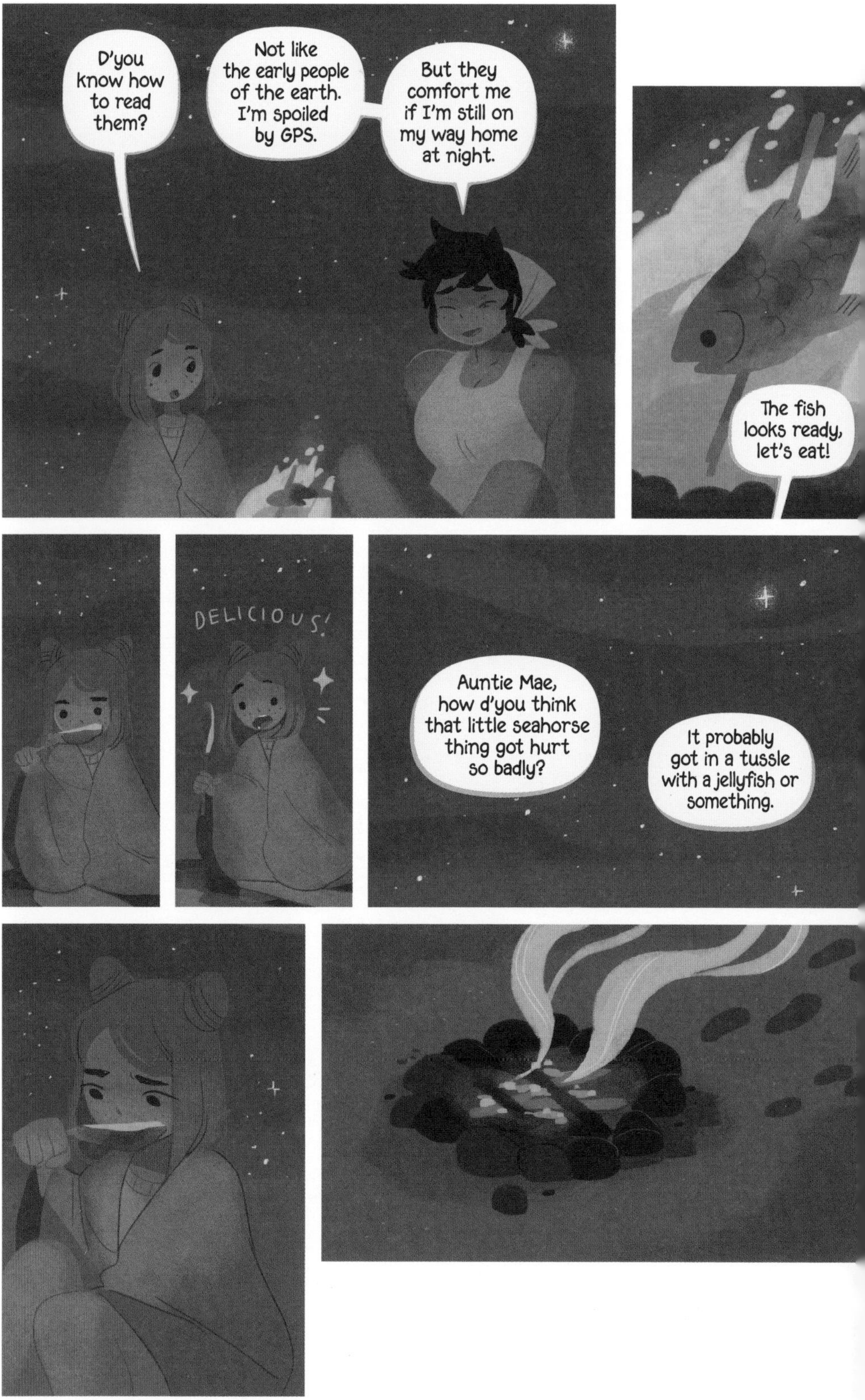
D'you know how to read them?
Not like the early people of the earth. I'm spoiled by GPS.
But they comfort me if I'm still on my way home at night.
The fish looks ready, let's eat!
DELICIOUS!
Auntie Mae, how d'you think that little seahorse thing got hurt so badly?
It probably got in a tussle with a jellyfish or something.

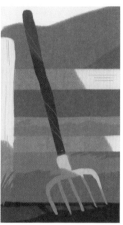

Look, Lana!

Swiss pumpkin!

Leave the dad jokes to Dad.

Thank goodness you had us put these tarps out, Mae.

We'd have lost a season's worth of food otherwise.

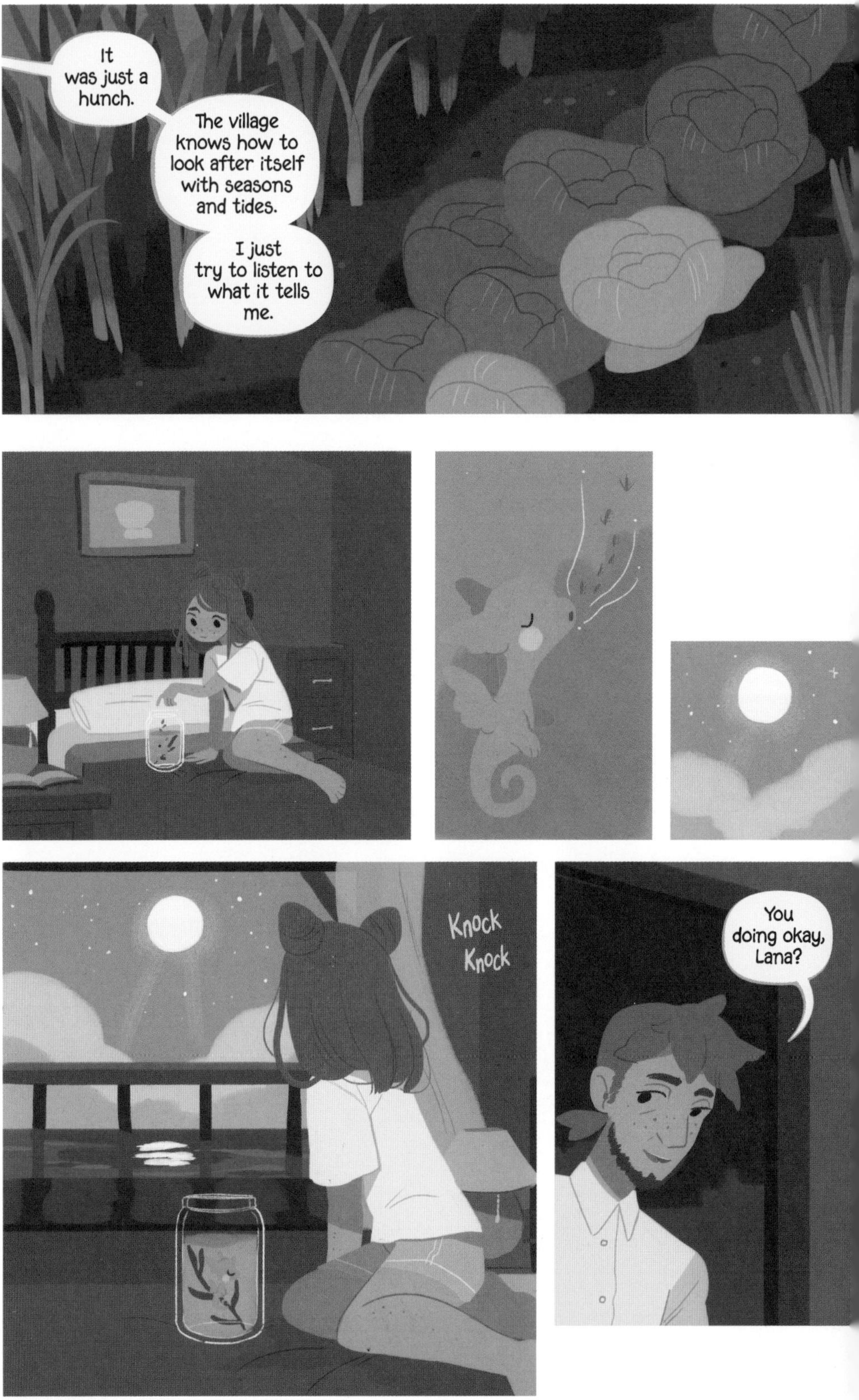
It was just a hunch.
The village knows how to look after itself with seasons and tides.
I just try to listen to what it tells me.
Knock Knock
You doing okay, Lana?

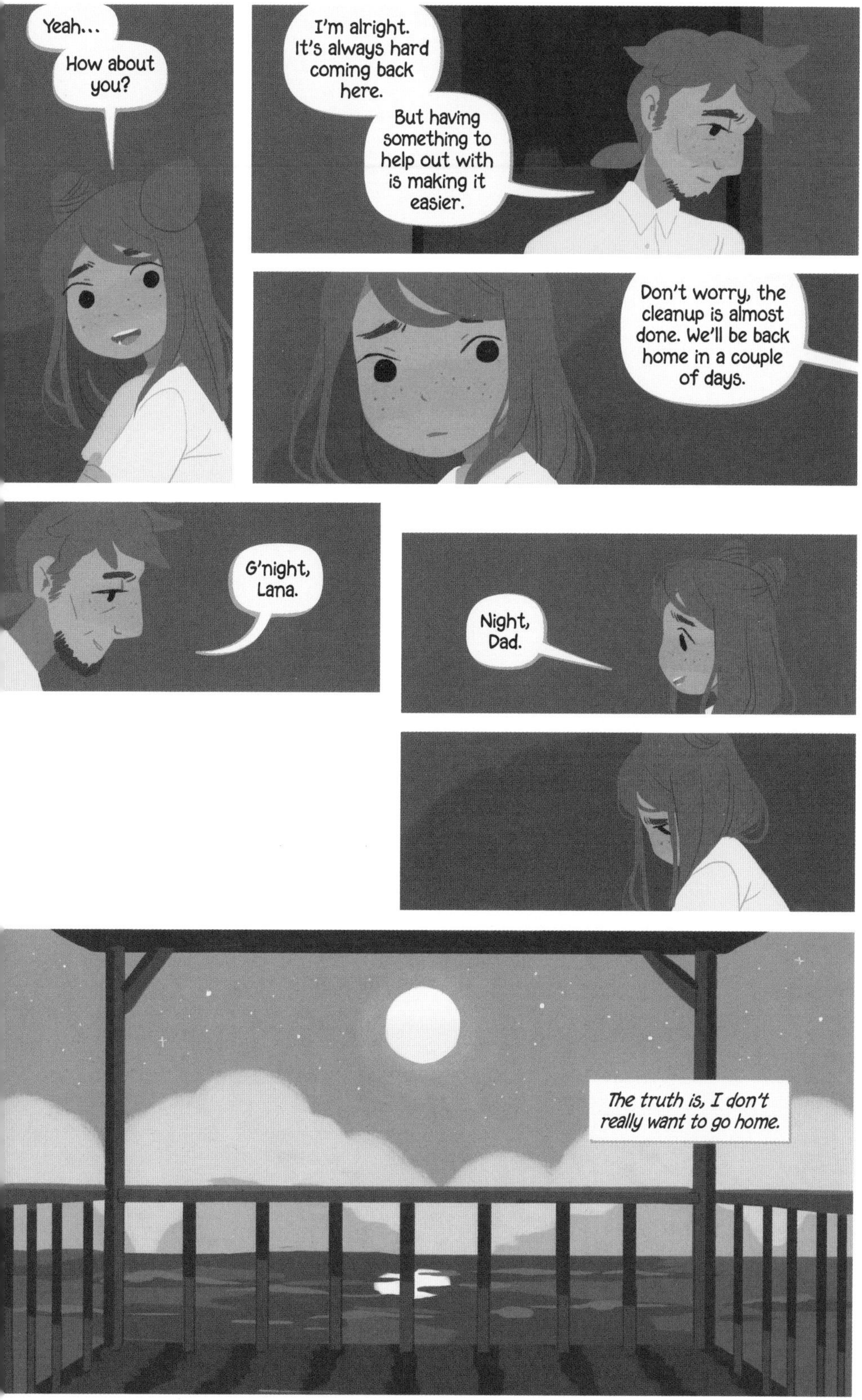
Yeah...
How about you?
I'm alright. It's always hard coming back here.
But having something to help out with is making it easier.
Don't worry, the cleanup is almost done. We'll be back home in a couple of days.
G'night, Lana.
Night, Dad.
The truth is, I don't really want to go home.

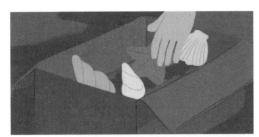

It was Dad who wanted us to move to the city...

He needed to.

$$m = \frac{y_2 - y_1}{x_2 - x_1}$$

Dad was busy trying to start our new life, and he was hurting too.

I needed help, but I didn't know how to ask.

I didn't know how to explain I needed help with the small things.

The things I never noticed before, until suddenly they took effort.

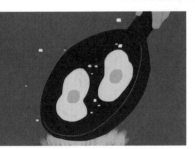

Sometimes I feel like I just want to go to sleep for a while, and wake up when I'm stronger or things are different somehow.

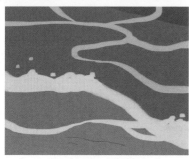

I don't want to go home.

I want to stay here, where Auntie Mae takes care of me.

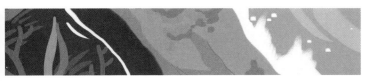

I want to feel like a kid, like a little fish in a rock pool.

I want Mom.

Thank you!

Everyone'll be happy to find the treasures they've lost!

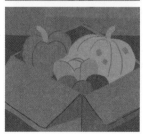

Auntie Mae! I saw more of those weird seahorses today!

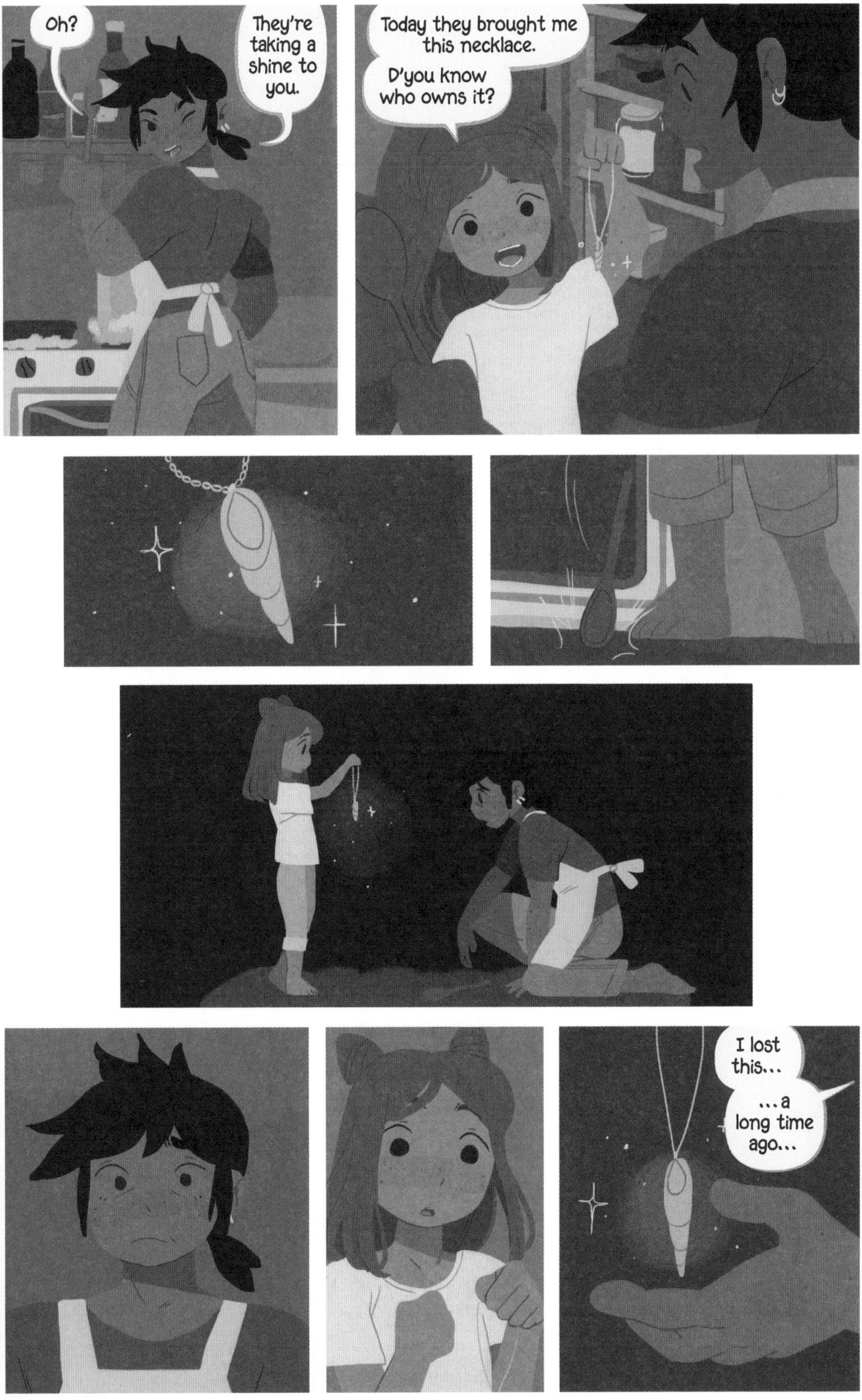
Oh?
They're taking a shine to you.
Today they brought me this necklace.
D'you know who owns it?
I lost this...
...a long time ago...

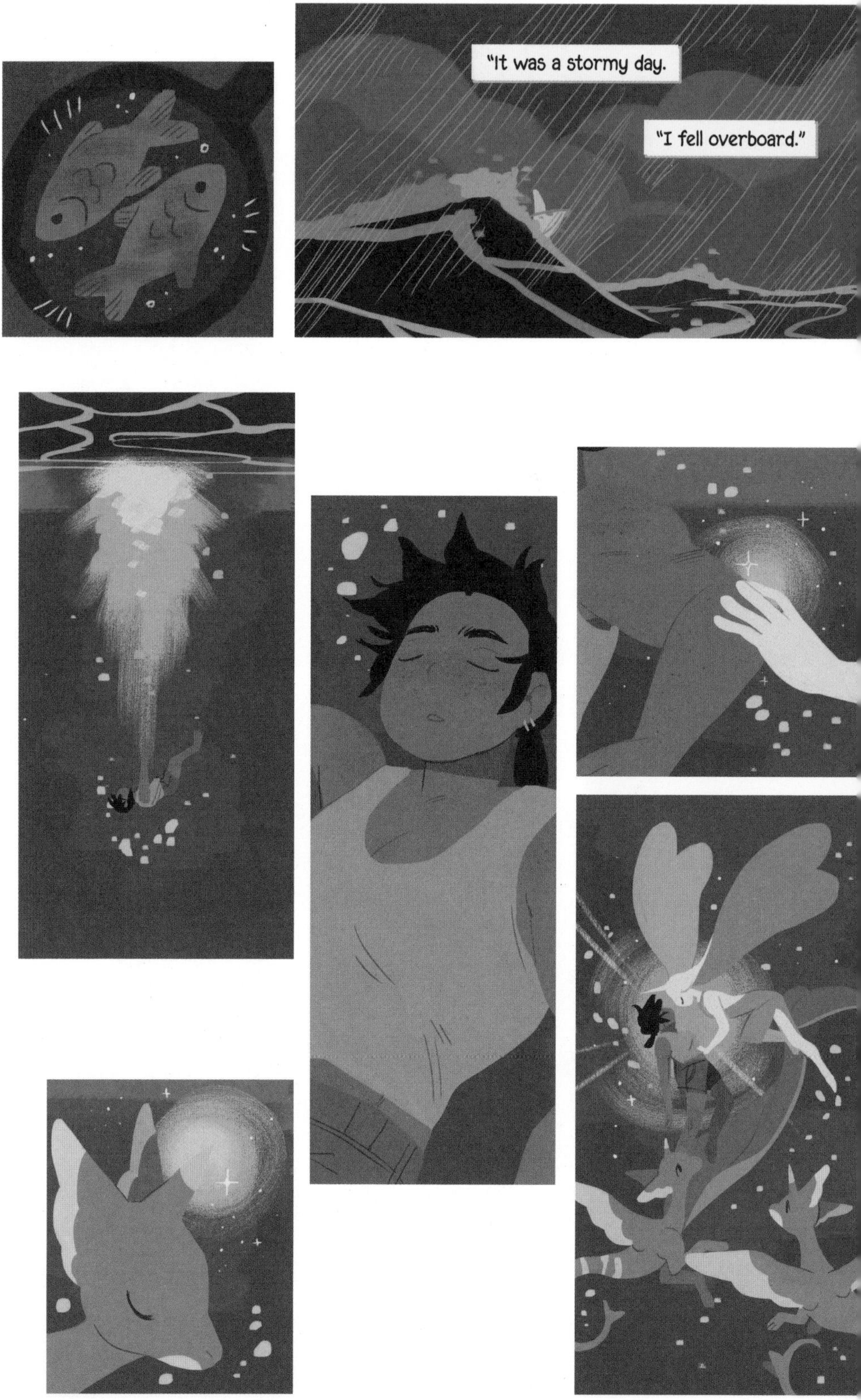
"It was a stormy day.
"I fell overboard."

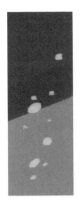

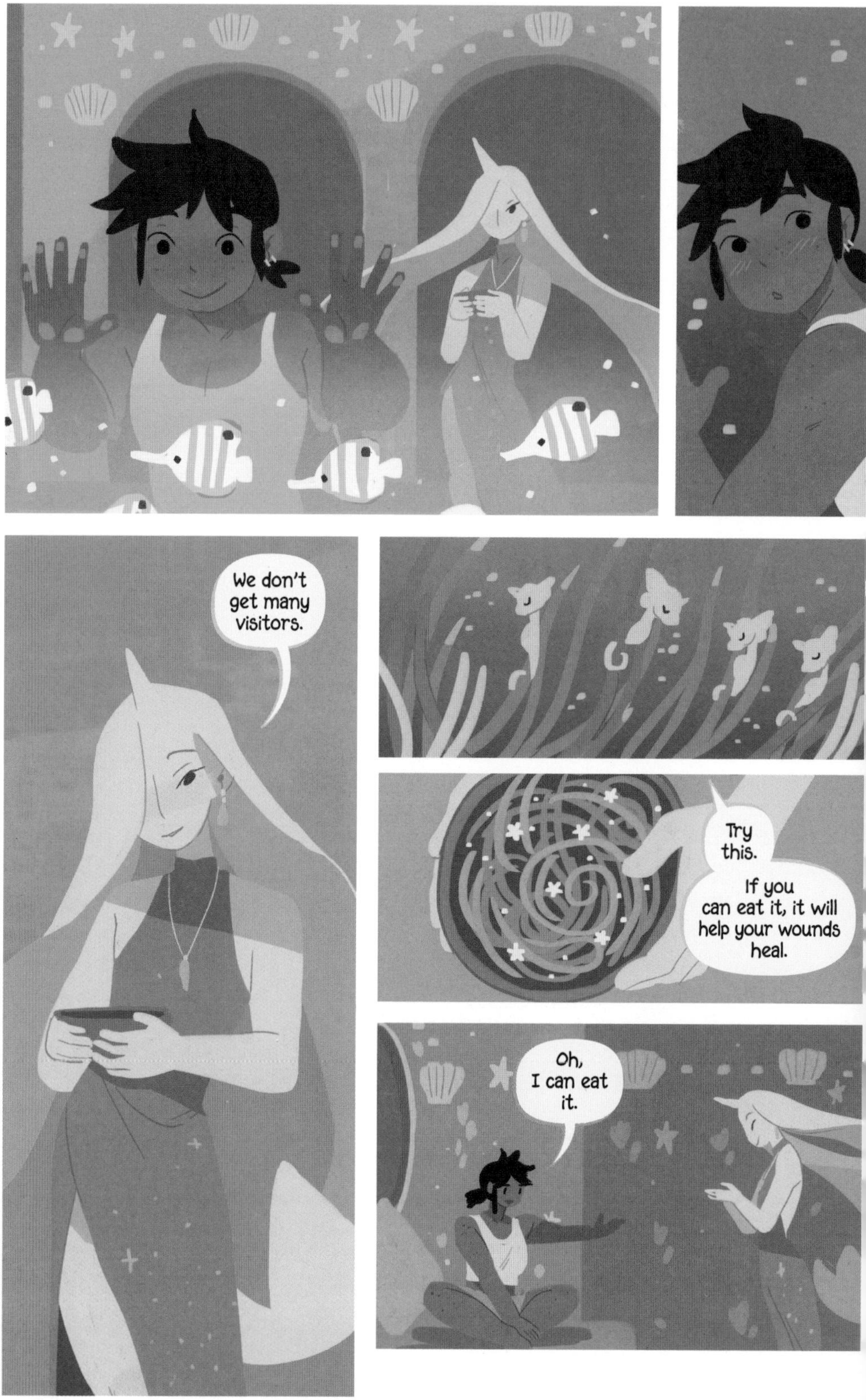
We don't get many visitors.
Try this.
If you can eat it, it will help your wounds heal.
Oh, I can eat it.

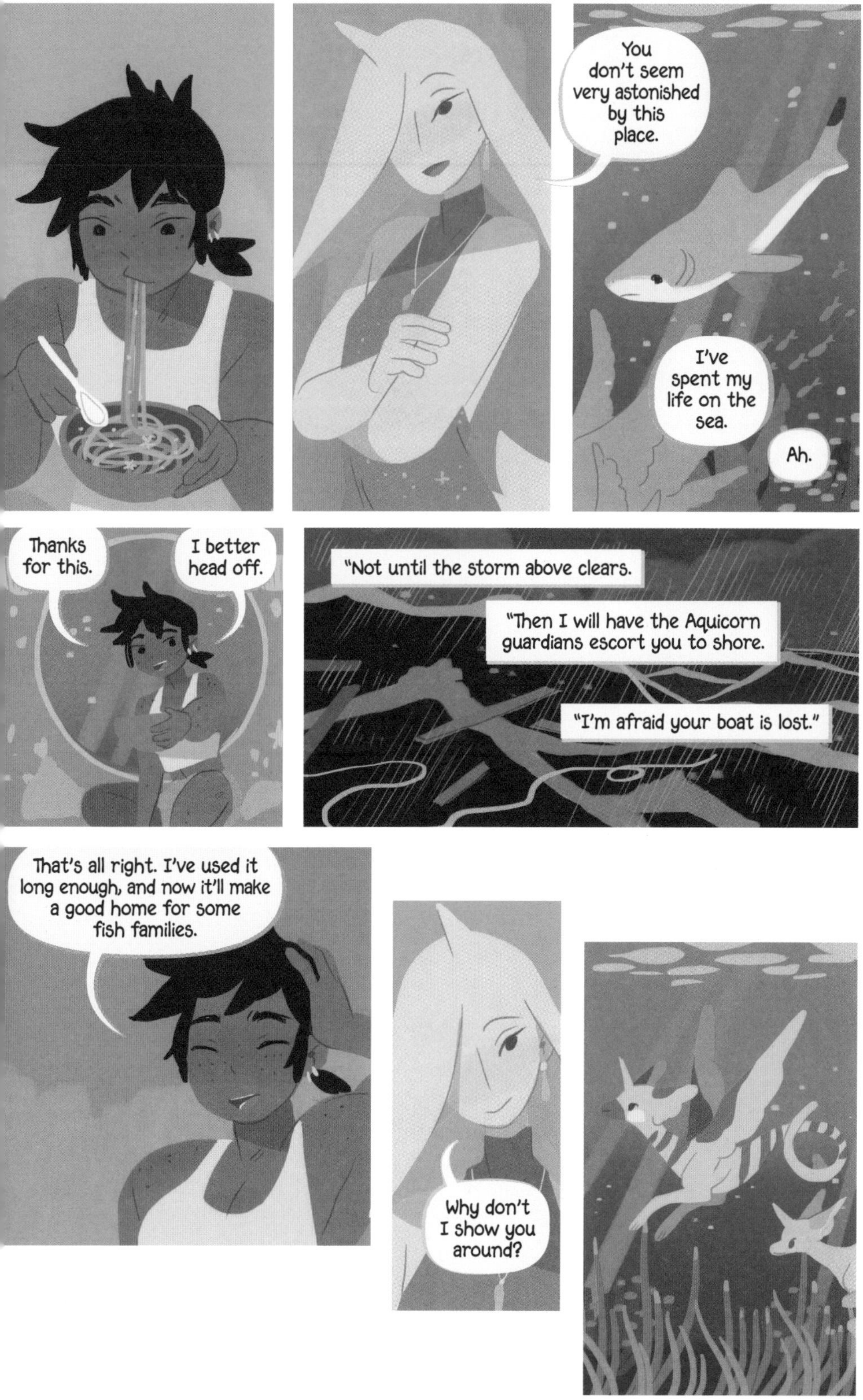
You don't seem very astonished by this place.
I've spent my life on the sea.
Ah.
Thanks for this.
I better head off.
"Not until the storm above clears.
"Then I will have the Aquicorn guardians escort you to shore.
"I'm afraid your boat is lost."
That's all right. I've used it long enough, and now it'll make a good home for some fish families.
Why don't I show you around?

I thought the snapper had moved on already!

They linger down here, as it's safe for them.

Safe from fishing nets.

We don't take more than they can give.

I appreciate that.

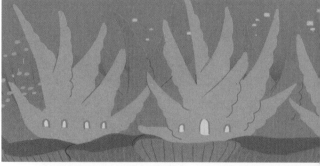

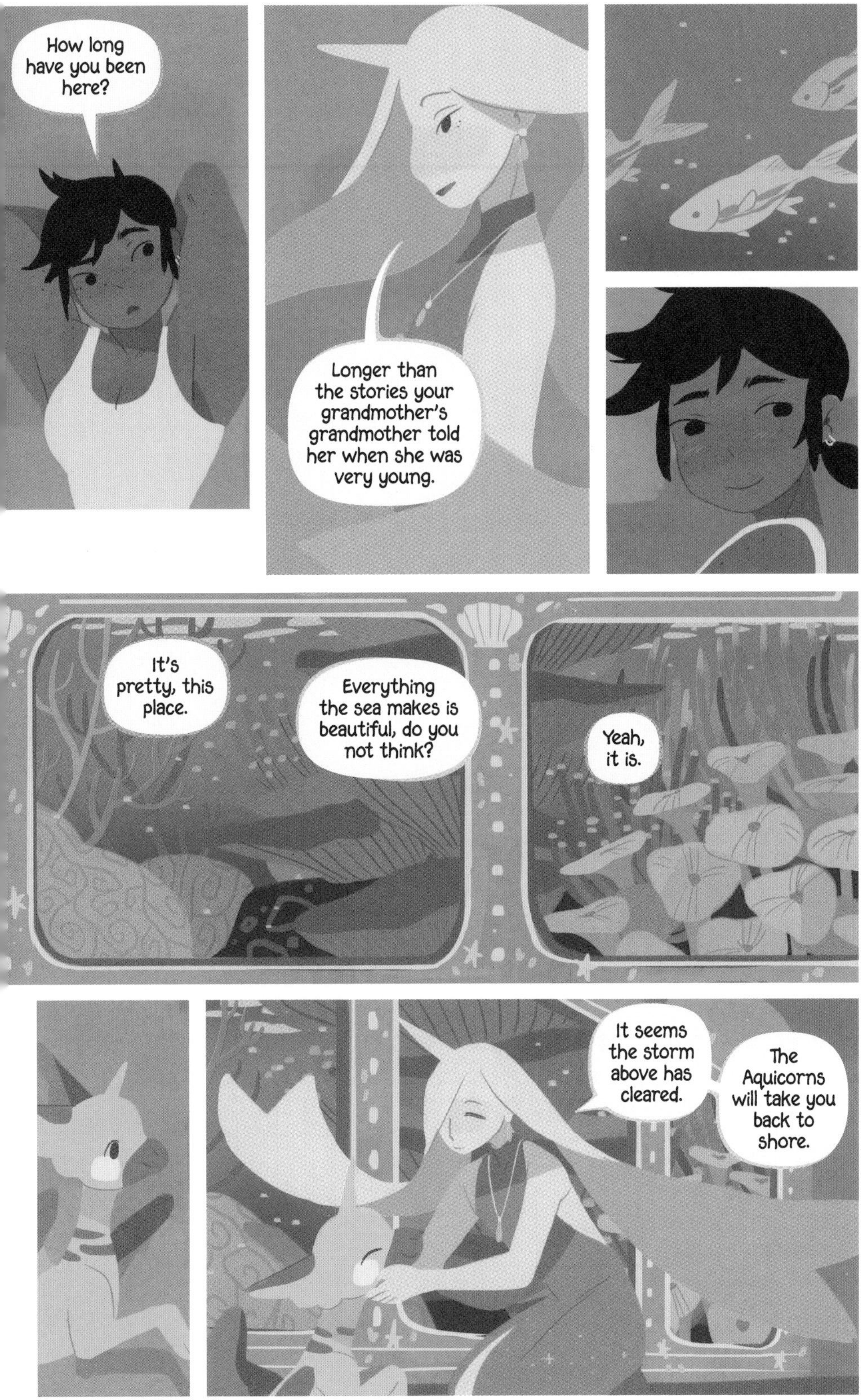
How long have you been here?
Longer than the stories your grandmother's grandmother told her when she was very young.
It's pretty, this place.
Everything the sea makes is beautiful, do you not think?
Yeah, it is.
It seems the storm above has cleared.
The Aquicorns will take you back to shore.

*Er,* if I wanted to come back, without falling overboard this time...

Here.

Wear this into the water, and the Aquicorns will guide you to me.

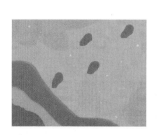

Who taught you to fish?

My mother, and her mother.

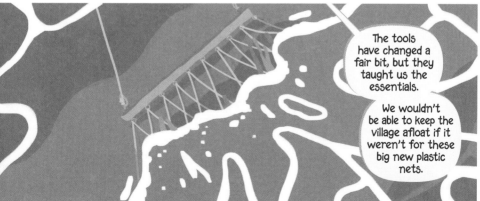
The tools have changed a fair bit, but they taught us the essentials.

We wouldn't be able to keep the village afloat if it weren't for these big new plastic nets.

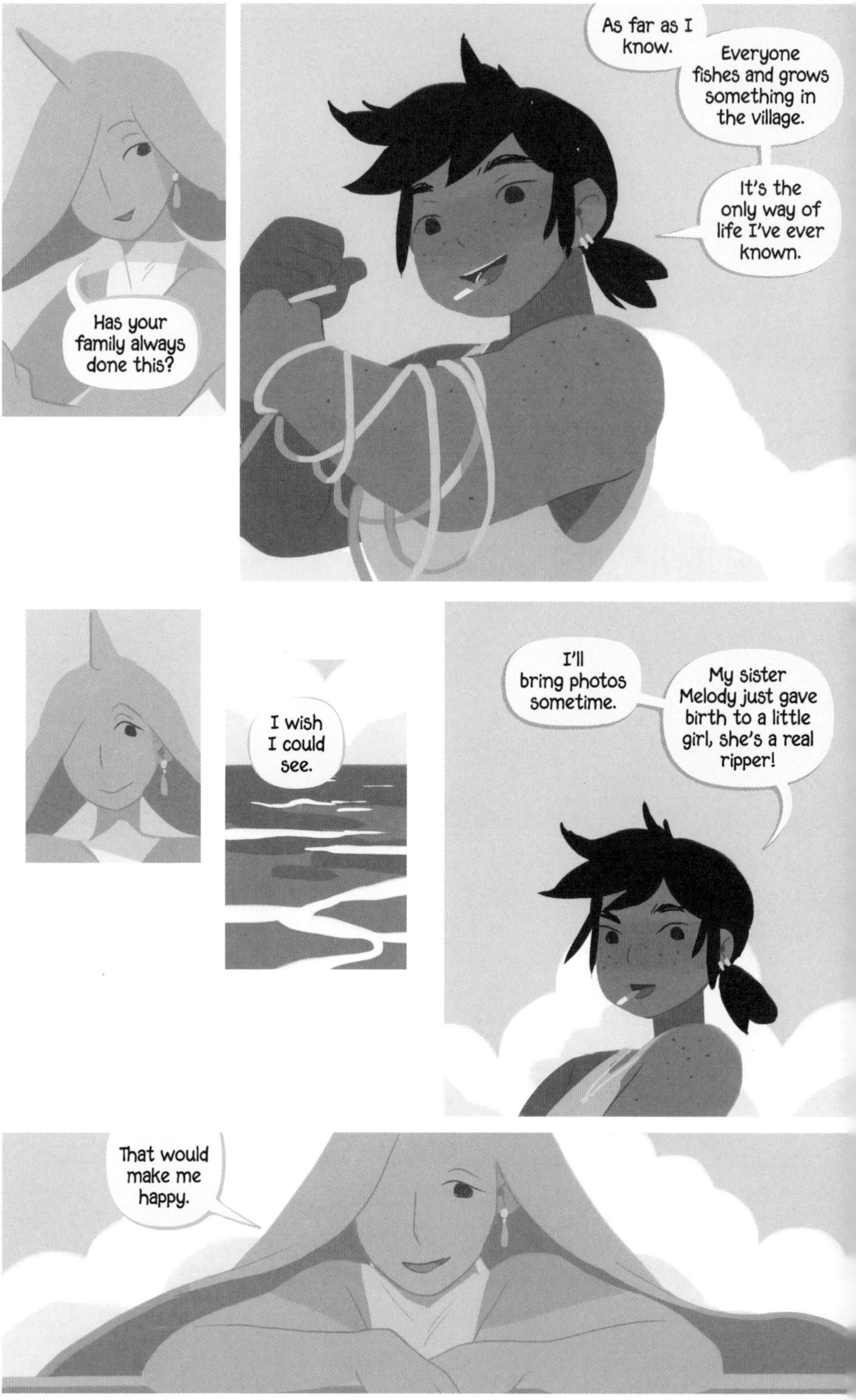
Has your family always done this?
As far as I know.
Everyone fishes and grows something in the village.
It's the only way of life I've ever known.
I wish I could see.
I'll bring photos sometime.
My sister Melody just gave birth to a little girl, she's a real ripper!
That would make me happy.

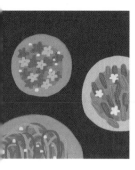

This is good! I didn't even know you could eat half this stuff.

I do not like to waste anything if I can help it.

Everything has a use.

Sometimes beautiful things are made through necessity.

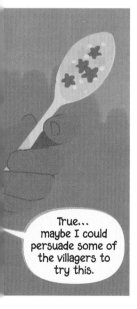

That might be a good idea.

There may not always be so many fish.

True... maybe I could persuade some of the villagers to try this.

Don't worry, we only take what we need.

And a bit to sell, but not much.

And then...

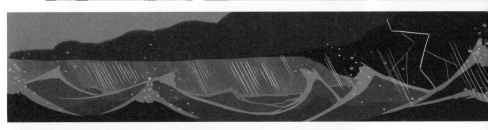

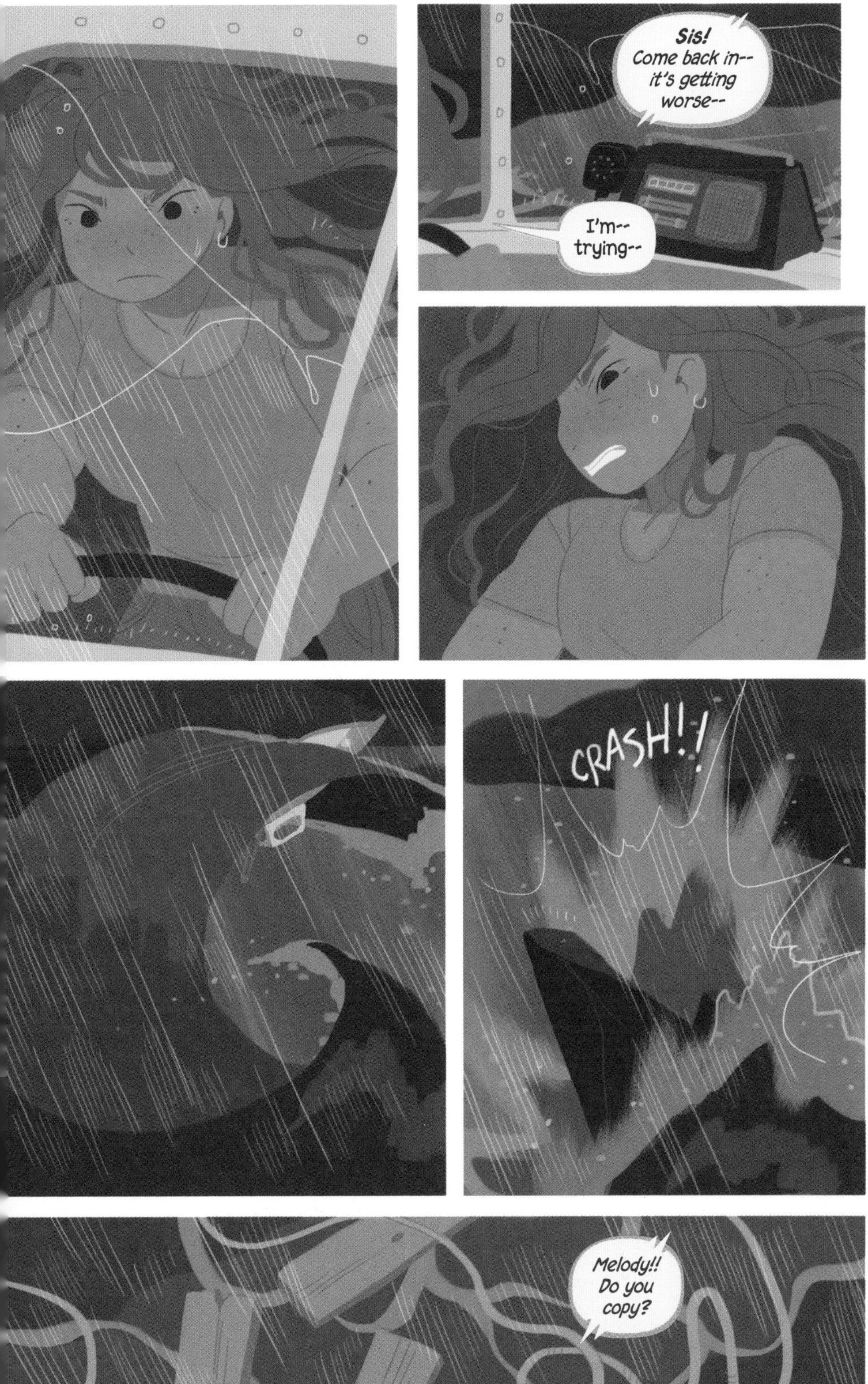
Sis!
Come back in--
it's getting
worse--
I'm--
trying--
CRASH!!
Melody!!
Do you
copy?

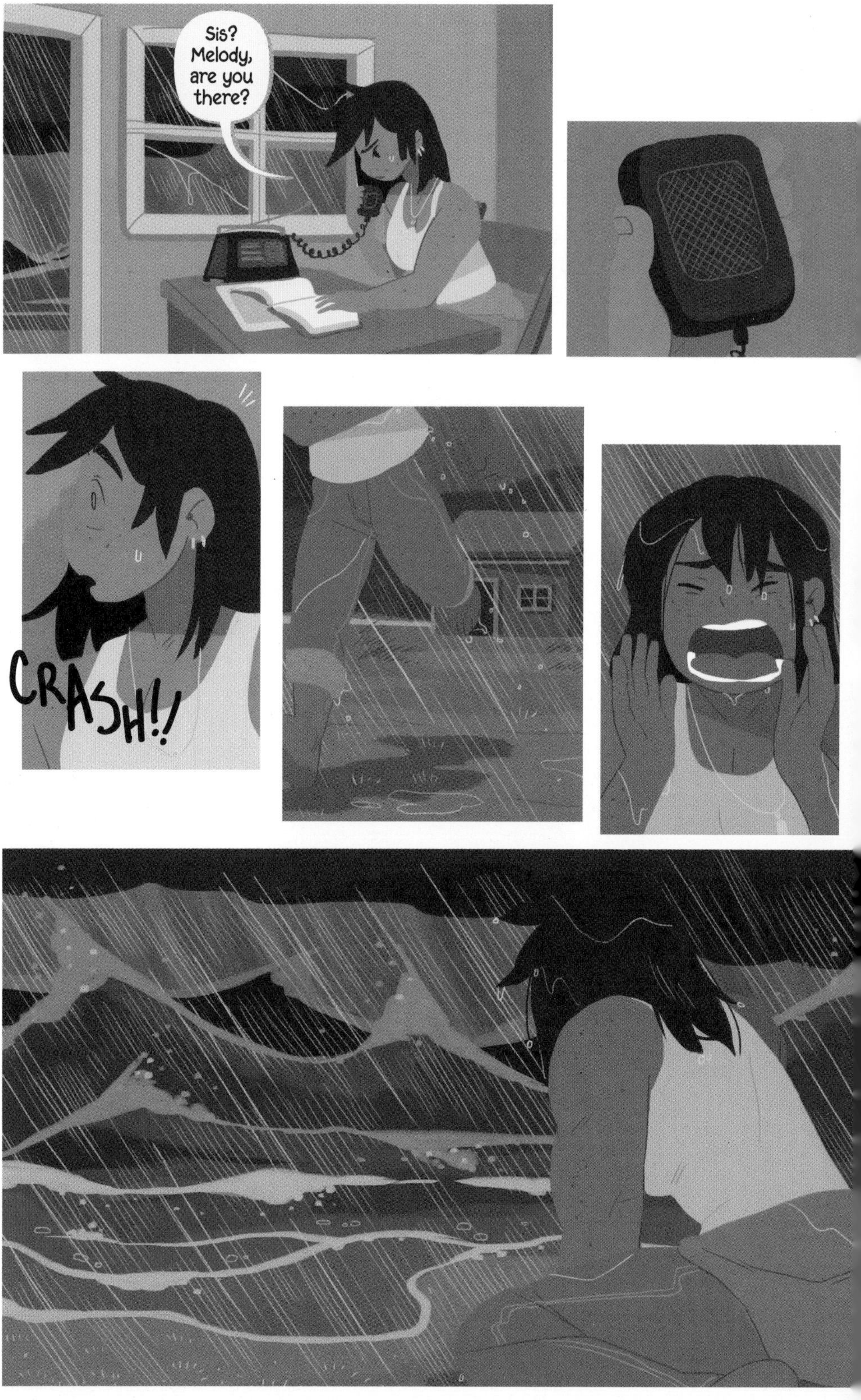
Sis? Melody, are you there?
CRASH!!

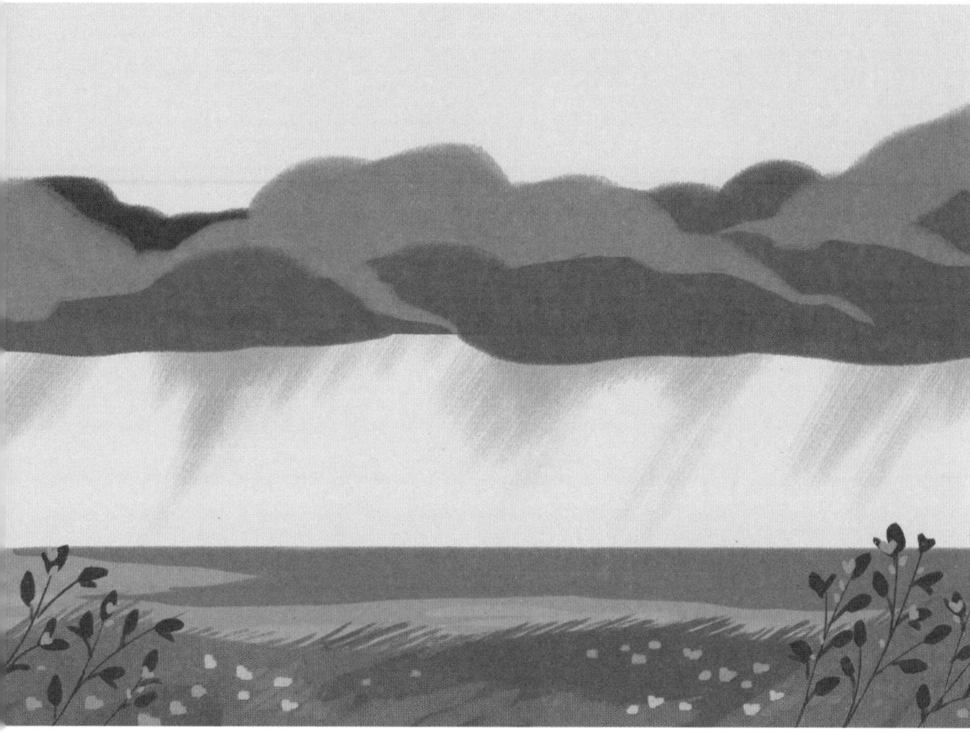

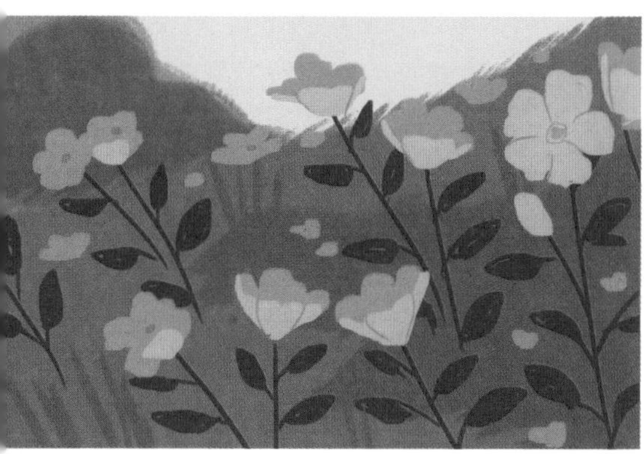

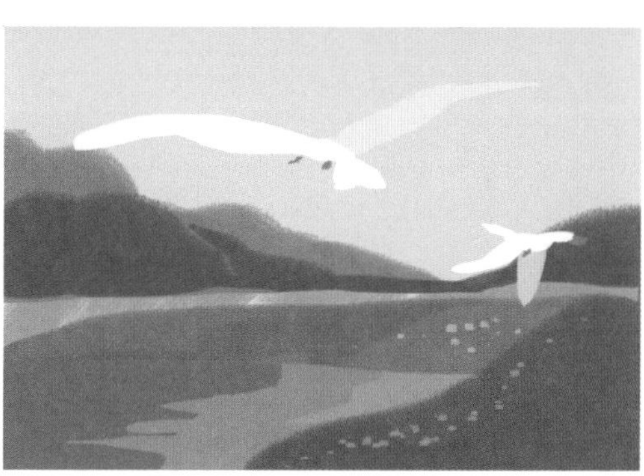

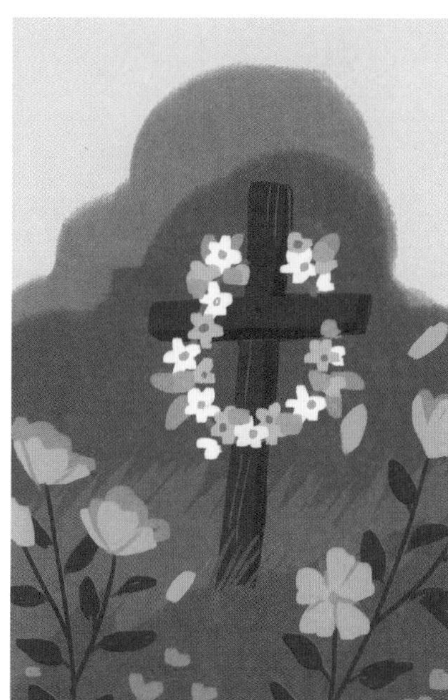

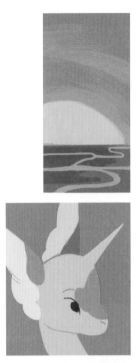

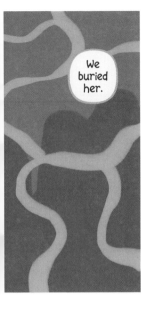

We buried her.

Thank you... for bringing her back to us.

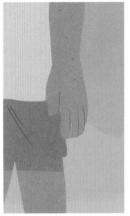

Don't be afraid of the sea.

Your dad is afraid of it now. I think he'll want to leave soon.

But this will always be your home, Lana.

And I will be too.

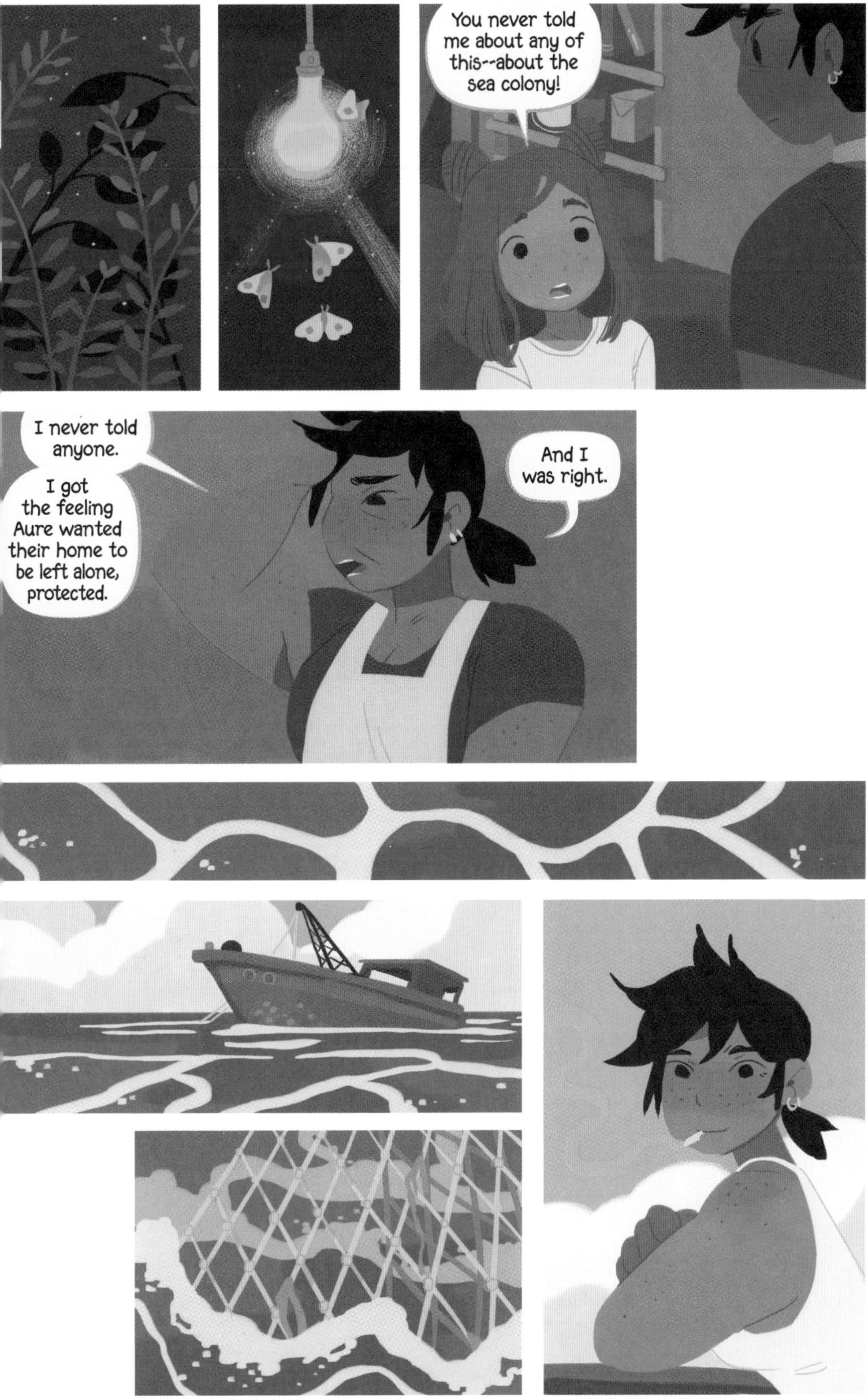
You never told me about any of this--about the sea colony!
I never told anyone.
I got the feeling Aure wanted their home to be left alone, protected.
And I was right.

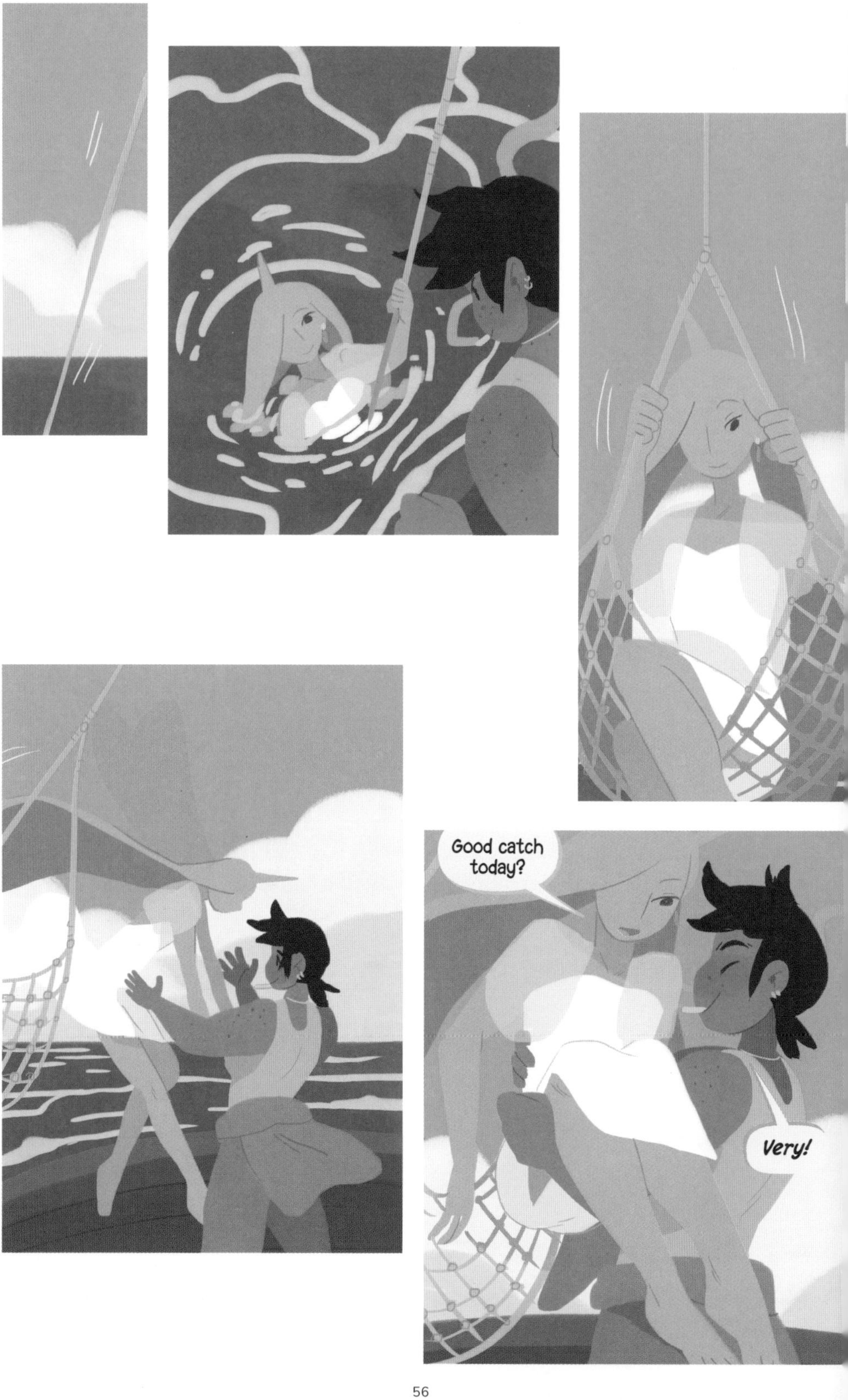
Good catch today?
Very!

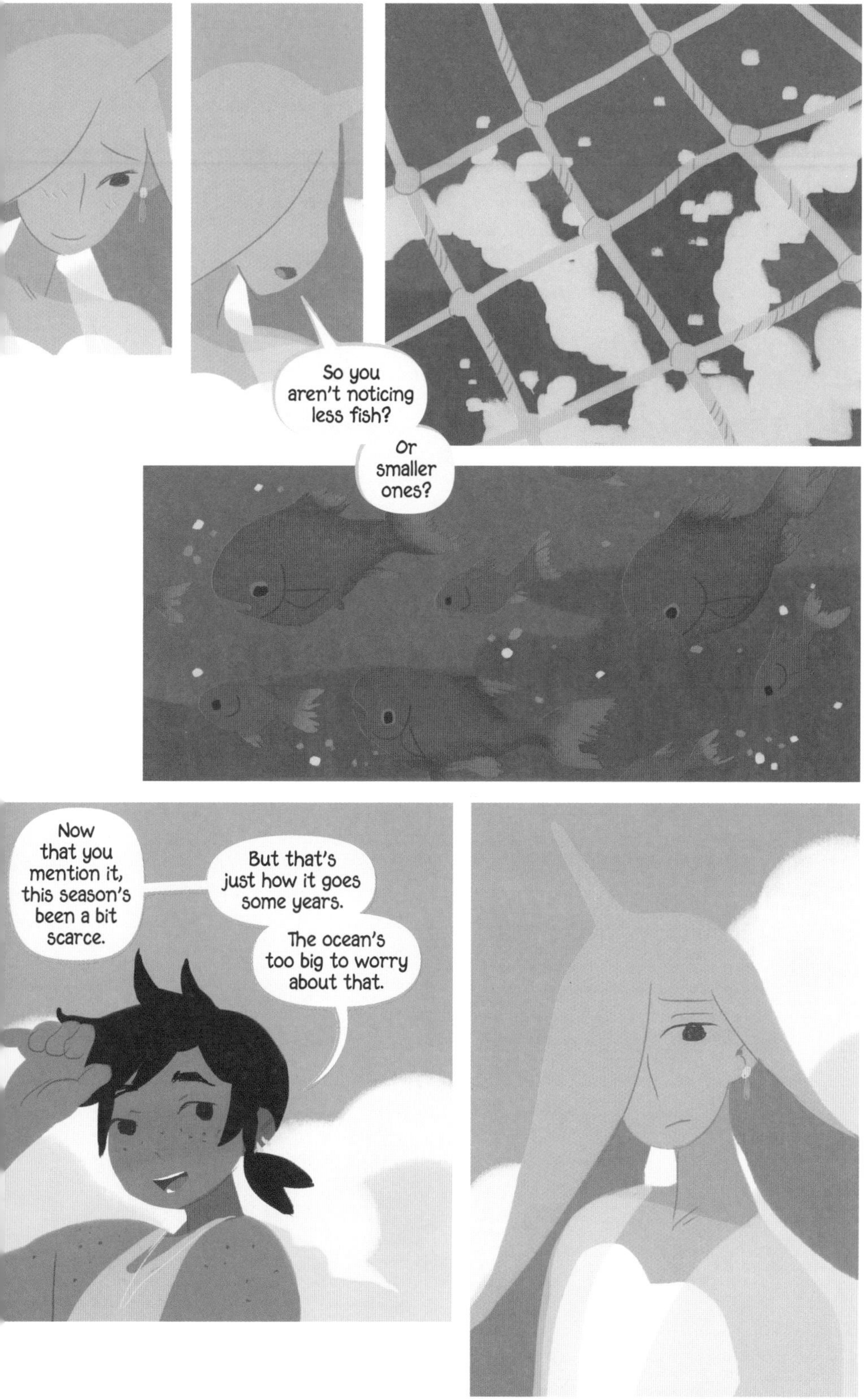
So you aren't noticing less fish?
Or smaller ones?
Now that you mention it, this season's been a bit scarce.
But that's just how it goes some years.
The ocean's too big to worry about that.

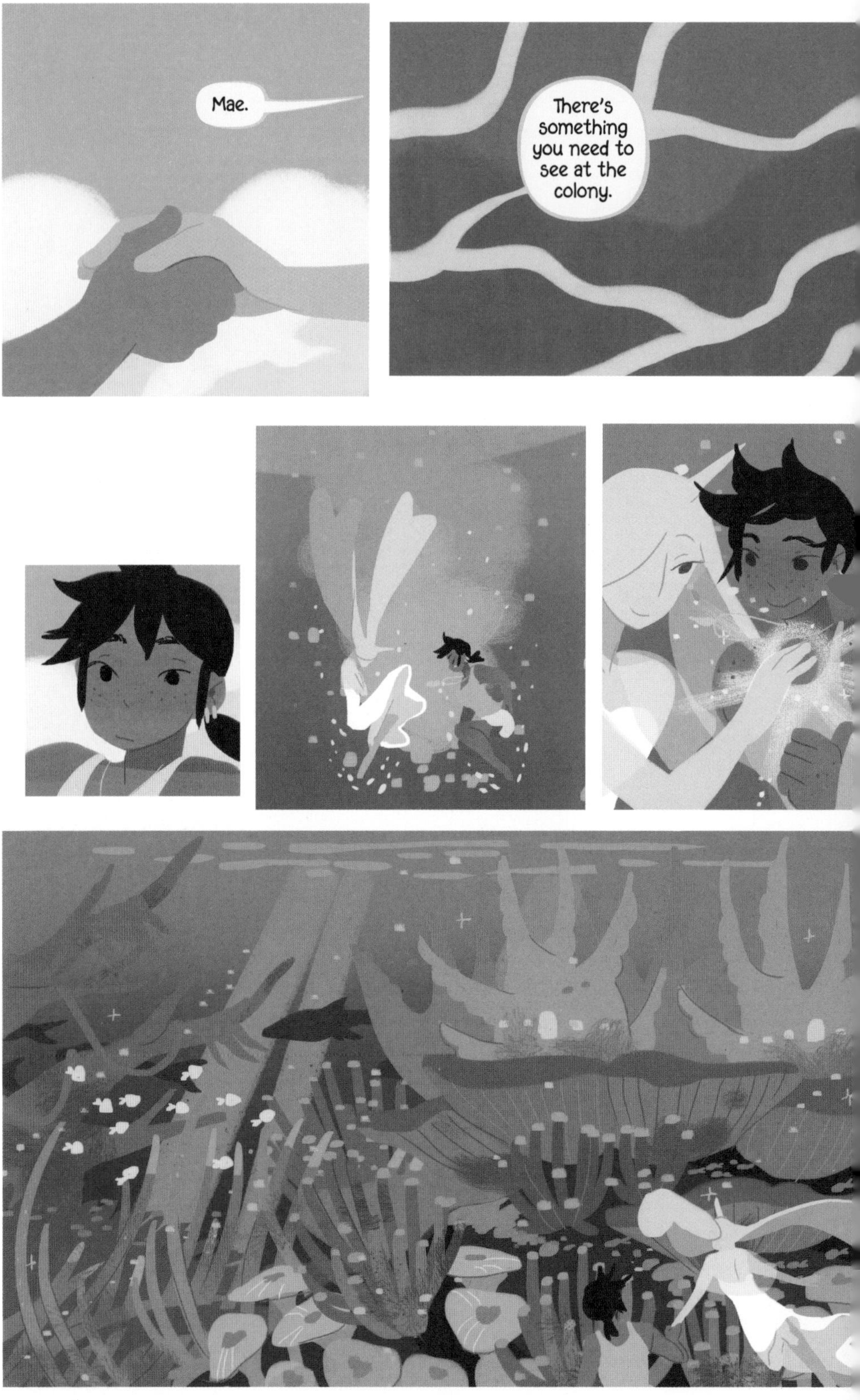
Mae.
There's something you need to see at the colony.

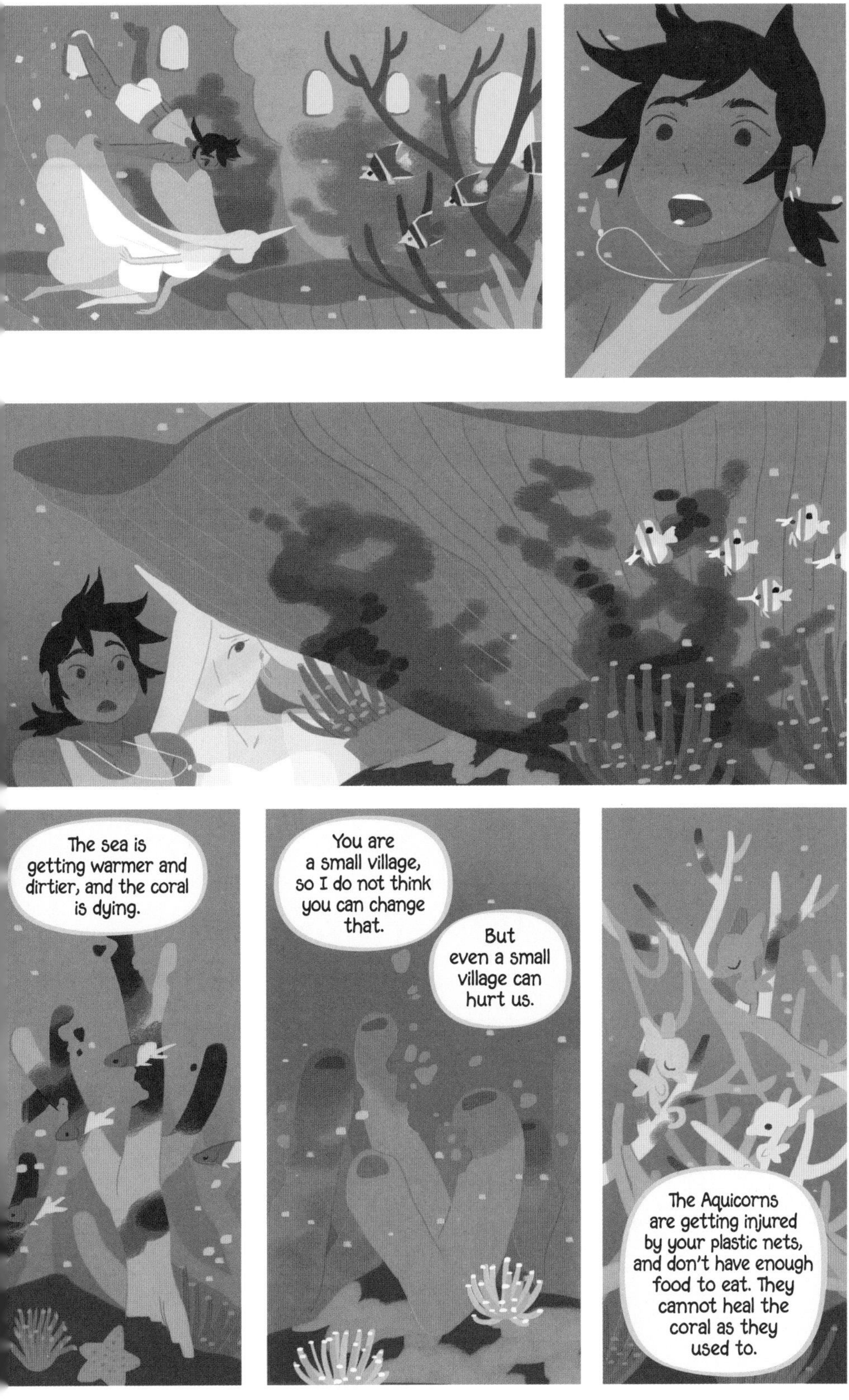
The sea is getting warmer and dirtier, and the coral is dying.
You are a small village, so I do not think you can change that.
But even a small village can hurt us.
The Aquicorns are getting injured by your plastic nets, and don't have enough food to eat. They cannot heal the coral as they used to.

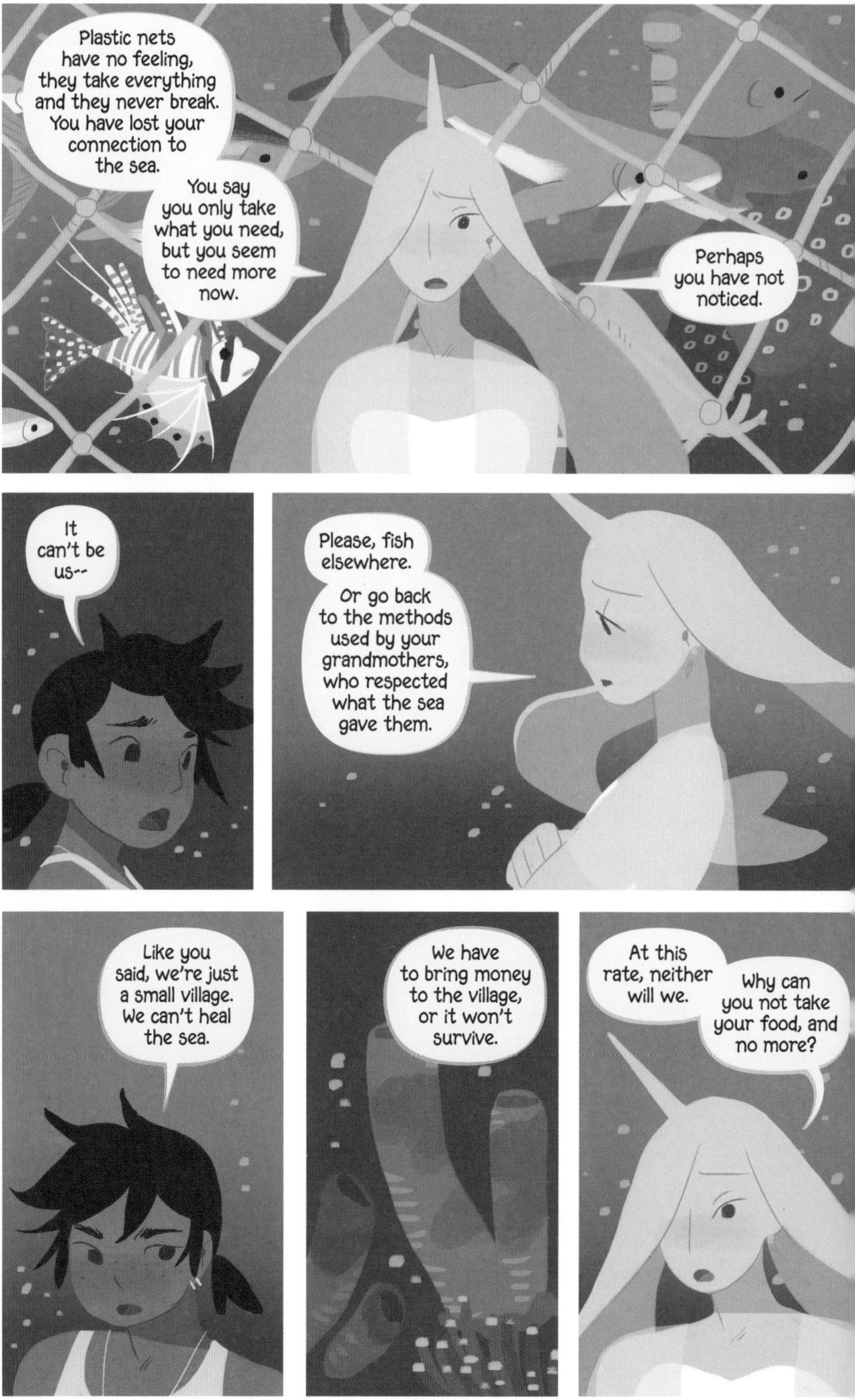
Plastic nets have no feeling, they take everything and they never break. You have lost your connection to the sea.
You say you only take what you need, but you seem to need more now.
Perhaps you have not noticed.
It can't be us--
Please, fish elsewhere.
Or go back to the methods used by your grandmothers, who respected what the sea gave them.
Like you said, we're just a small village. We can't heal the sea.
We have to bring money to the village, or it won't survive.
At this rate, neither will we.
Why can you not take your food, and no more?

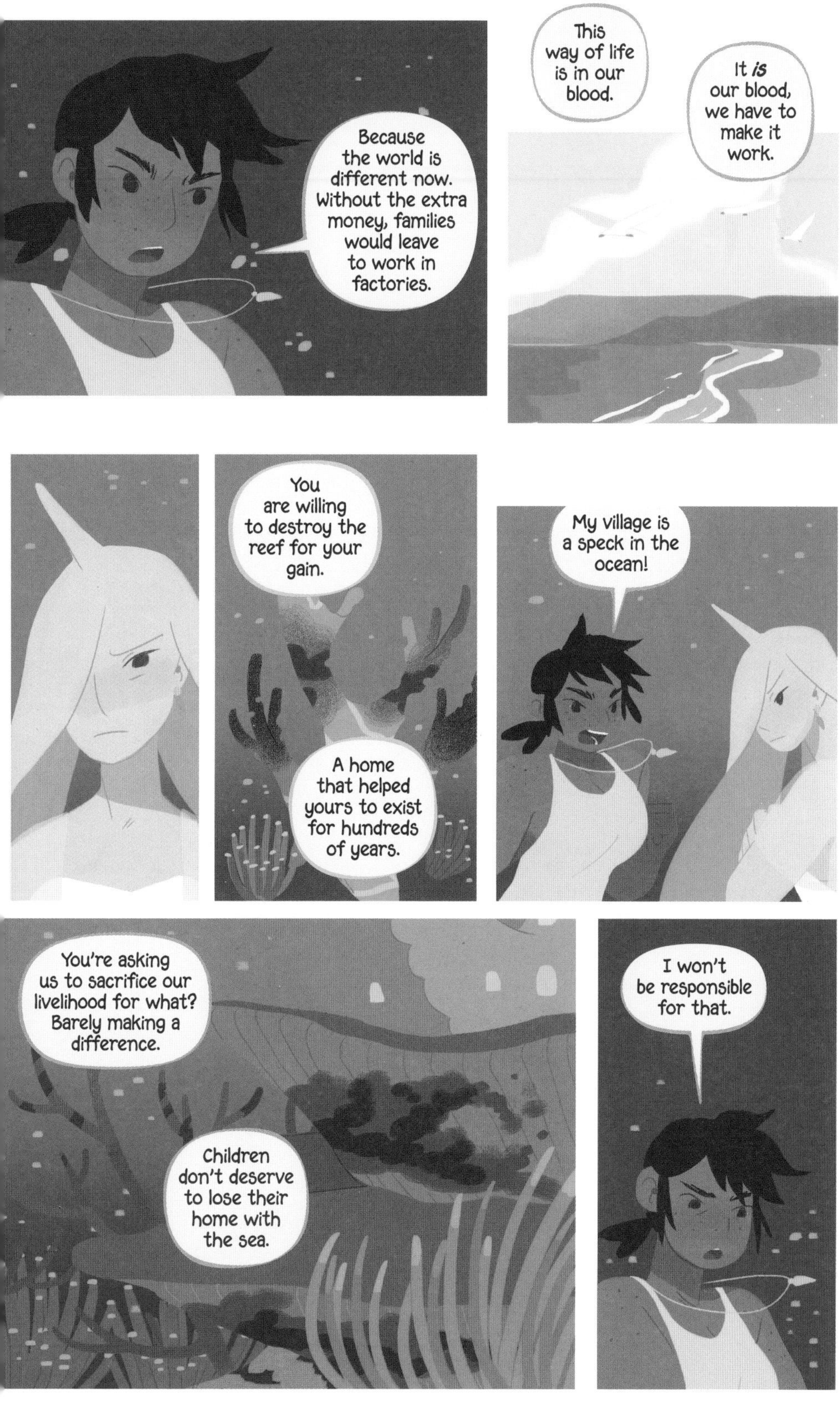

Because the world is different now. Without the extra money, families would leave to work in factories.
This way of life is in our blood.
It *is* our blood, we have to make it work.
You are willing to destroy the reef for your gain.
A home that helped yours to exist for hundreds of years.
My village is a speck in the ocean!
You're asking us to sacrifice our livelihood for what? Barely making a difference.
Children don't deserve to lose their home with the sea.
I won't be responsible for that.

I never imagined you could be so heartless.

My heart is with my village.

Then you should stay there.

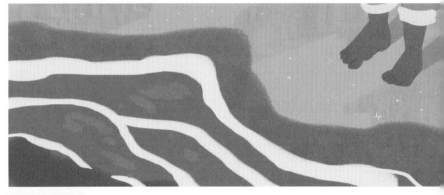

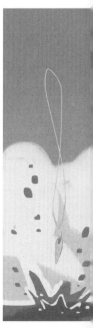

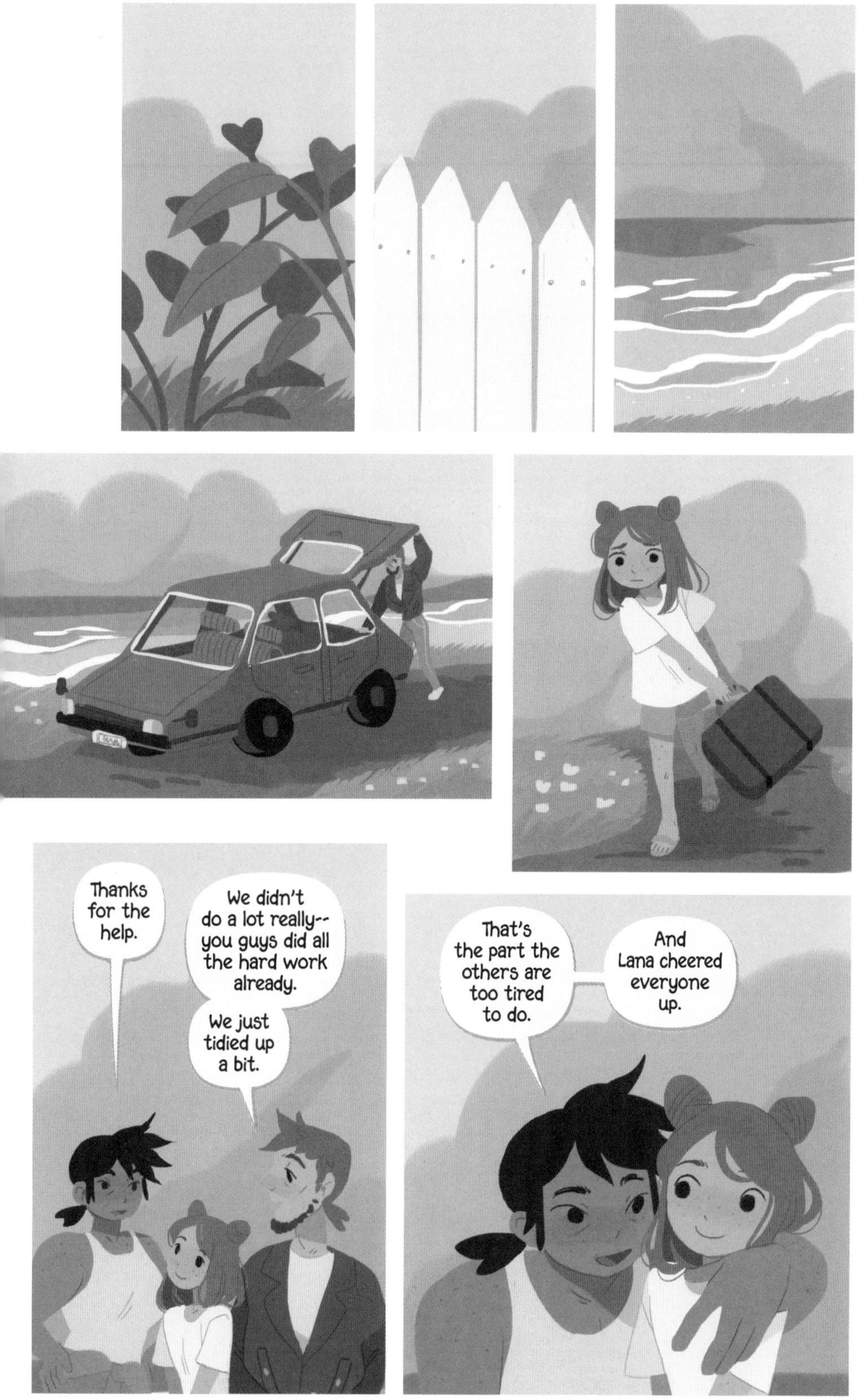

Thanks for the help.
We didn't do a lot really-- you guys did all the hard work already.
We just tidied up a bit.
That's the part the others are too tired to do.
And Lana cheered everyone up.

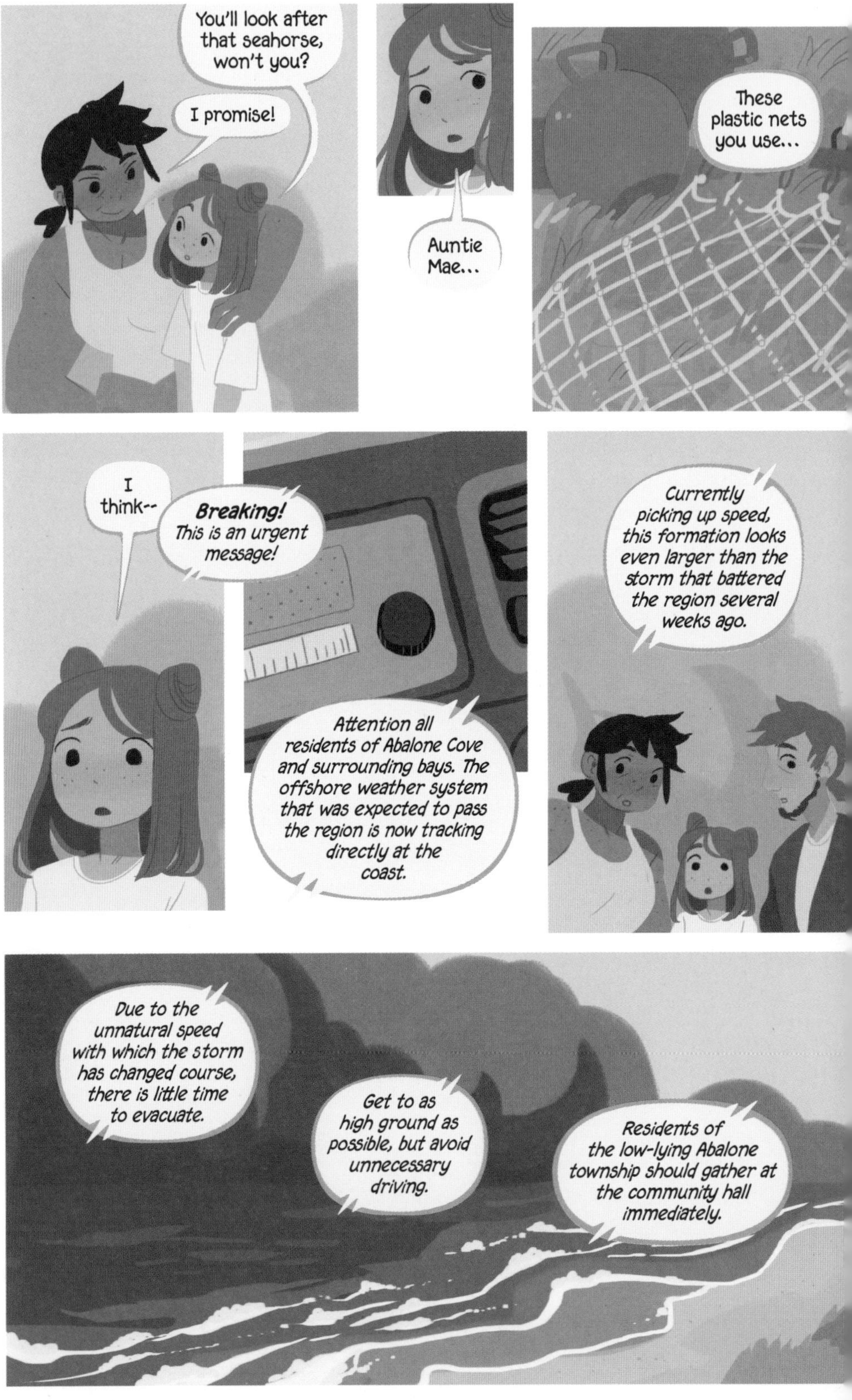

You'll look after that seahorse, won't you?
I promise!
Auntie Mae...
These plastic nets you use...
I think--
Breaking! This is an urgent message!
Attention all residents of Abalone Cove and surrounding bays. The offshore weather system that was expected to pass the region is now tracking directly at the coast.
Currently picking up speed, this formation looks even larger than the storm that battered the region several weeks ago.
Due to the unnatural speed with which the storm has changed course, there is little time to evacuate.
Get to as high ground as possible, but avoid unnecessary driving.
Residents of the low-lying Abalone township should gather at the community hall immediately.

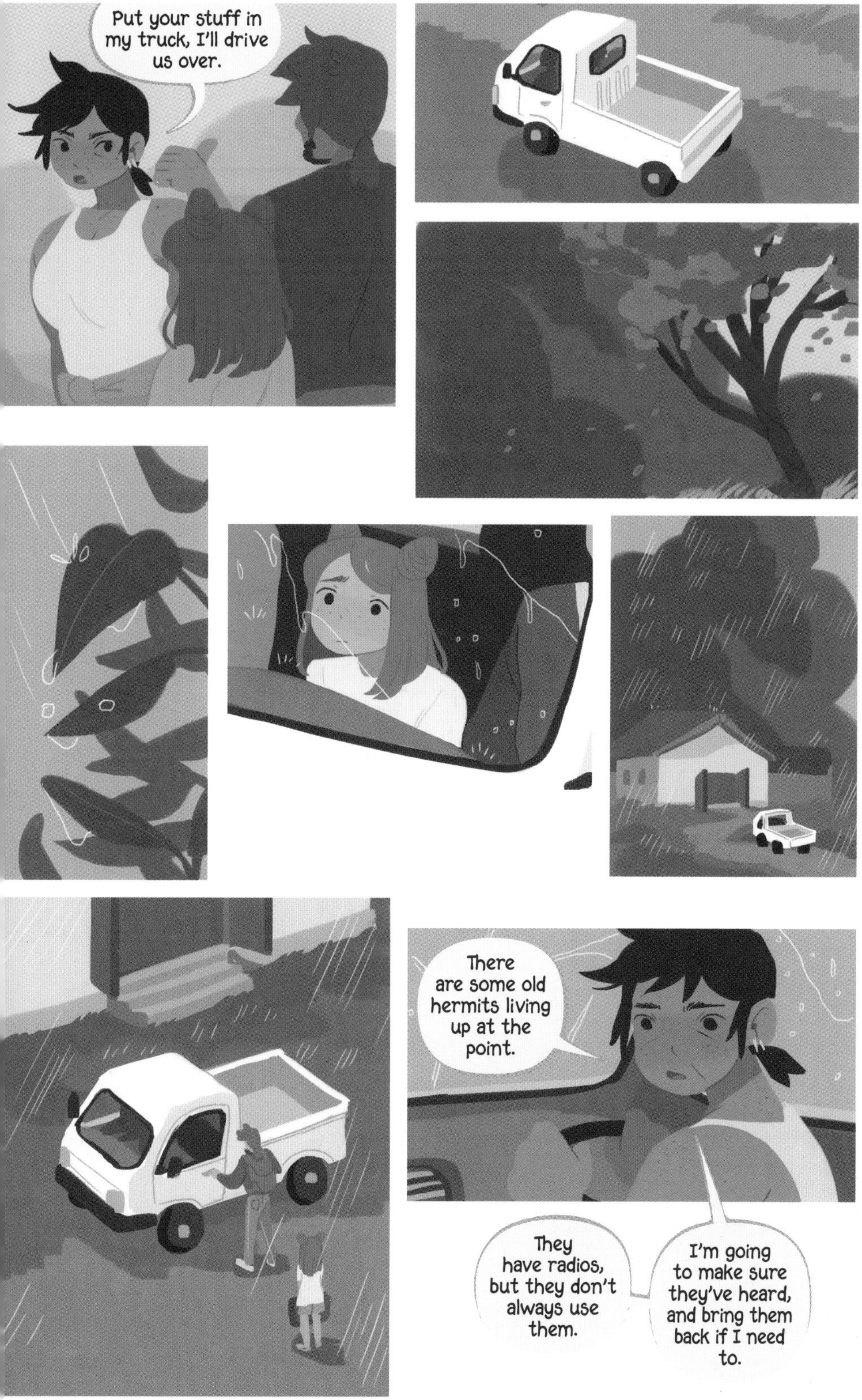
Put your stuff in my truck, I'll drive us over.
There are some old hermits living up at the point.
They have radios, but they don't always use them.
I'm going to make sure they've heard, and bring them back if I need to.

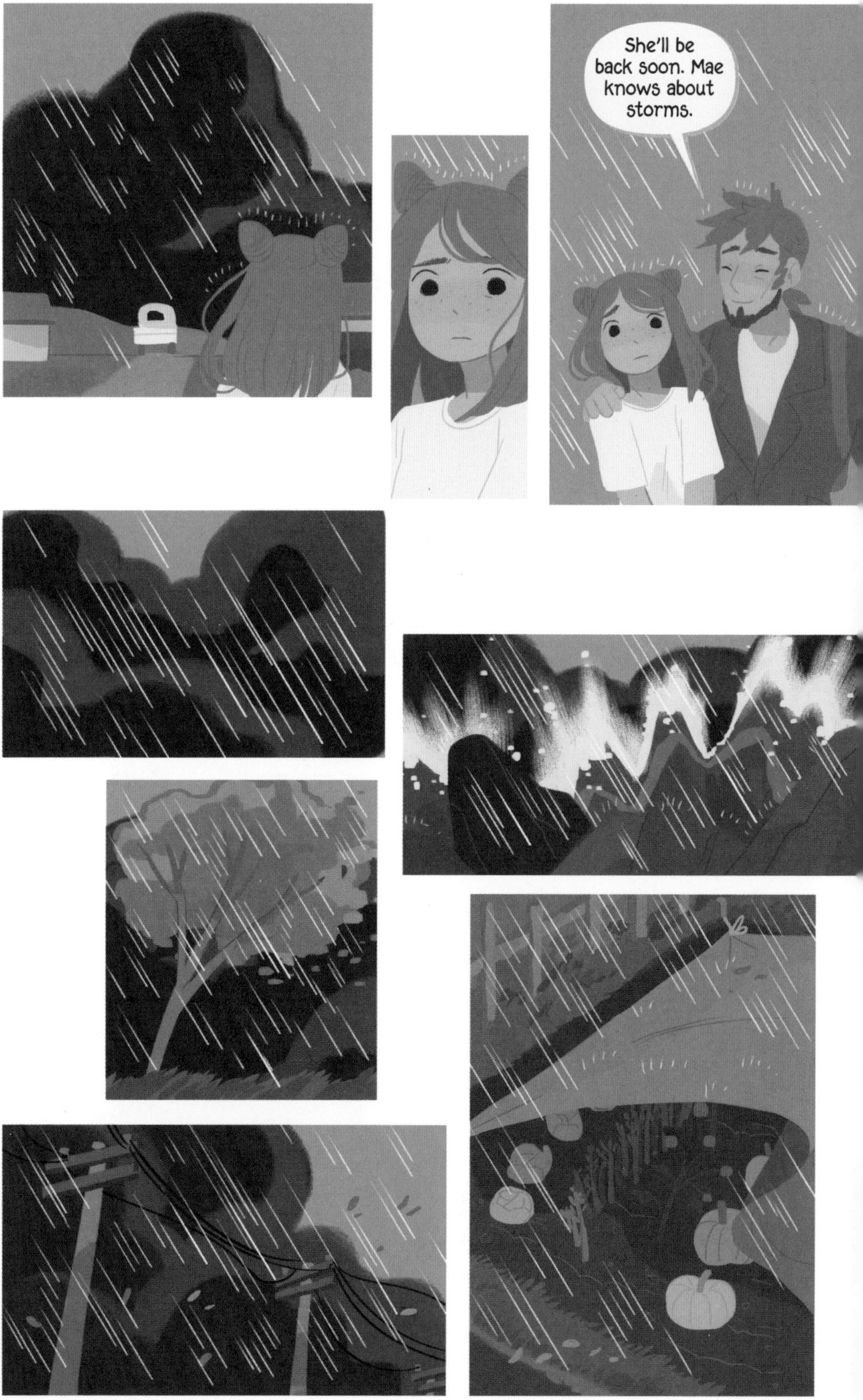
She'll be back soon. Mae knows about storms.

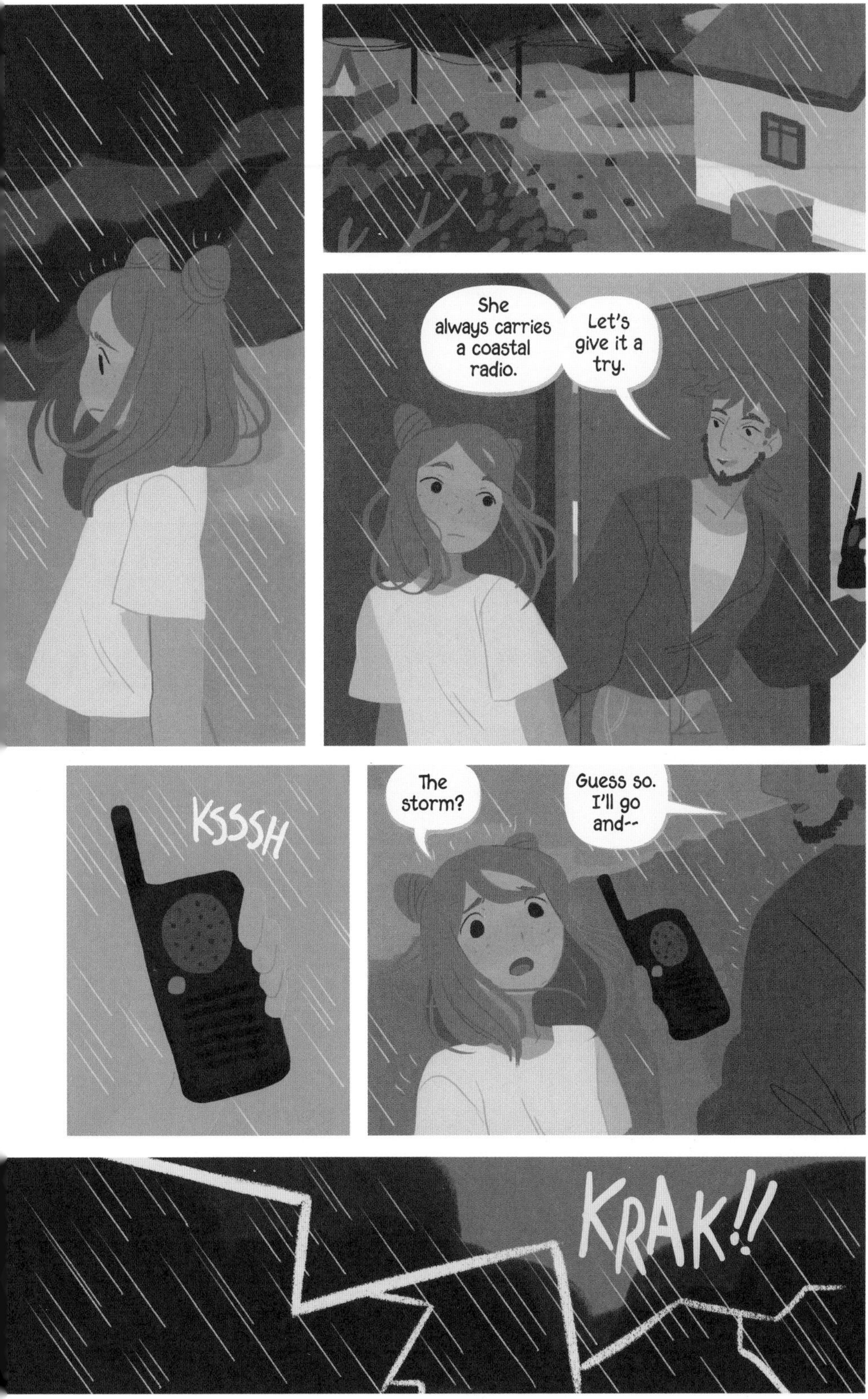
She always carries a coastal radio.
Let's give it a try.
KSSSH
The storm?
Guess so. I'll go and--
KRAK!!

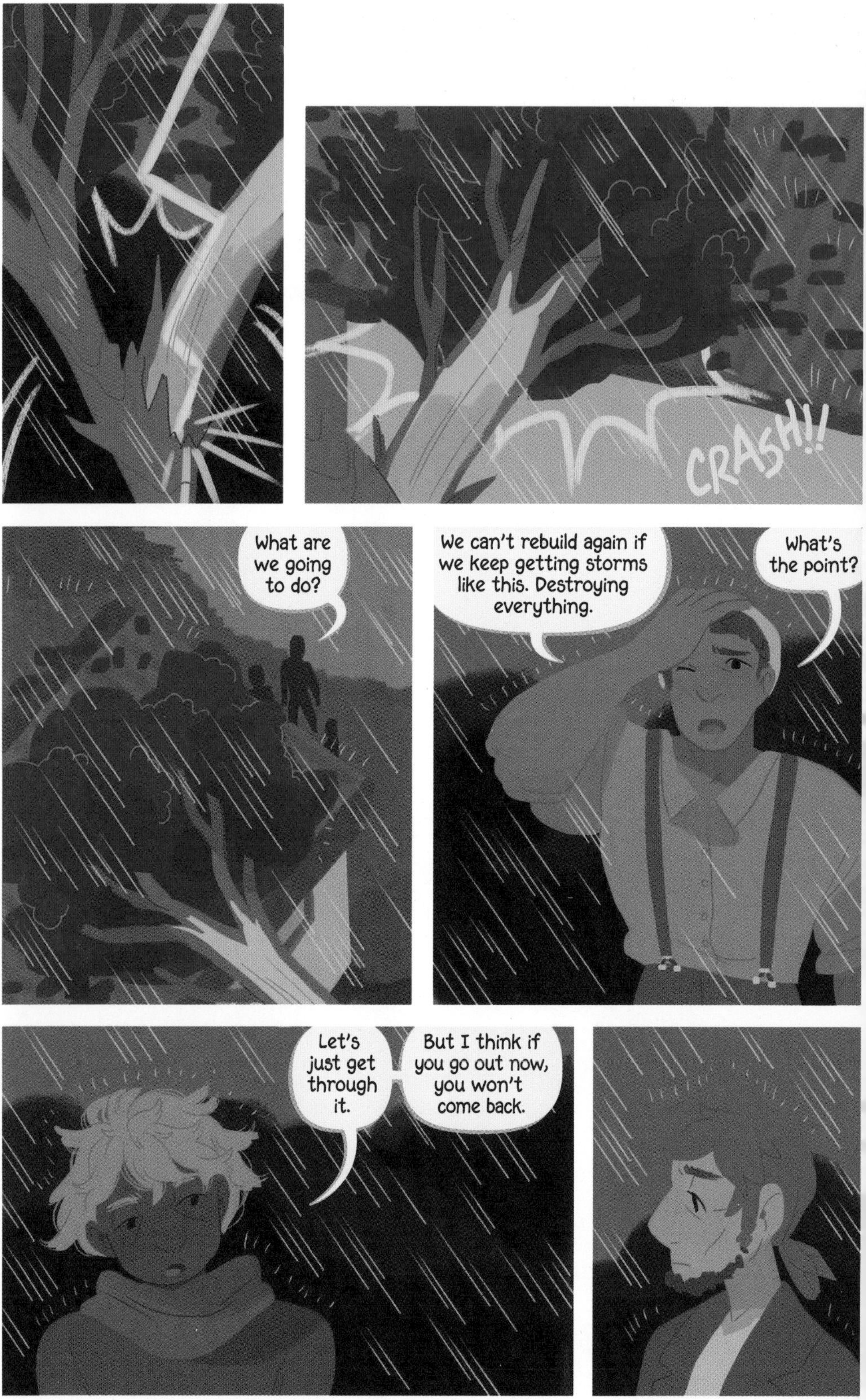
CRASH!!
What are we going to do?
We can't rebuild again if we keep getting storms like this. Destroying everything.
What's the point?
Let's just get through it.
But I think if you go out now, you won't come back.

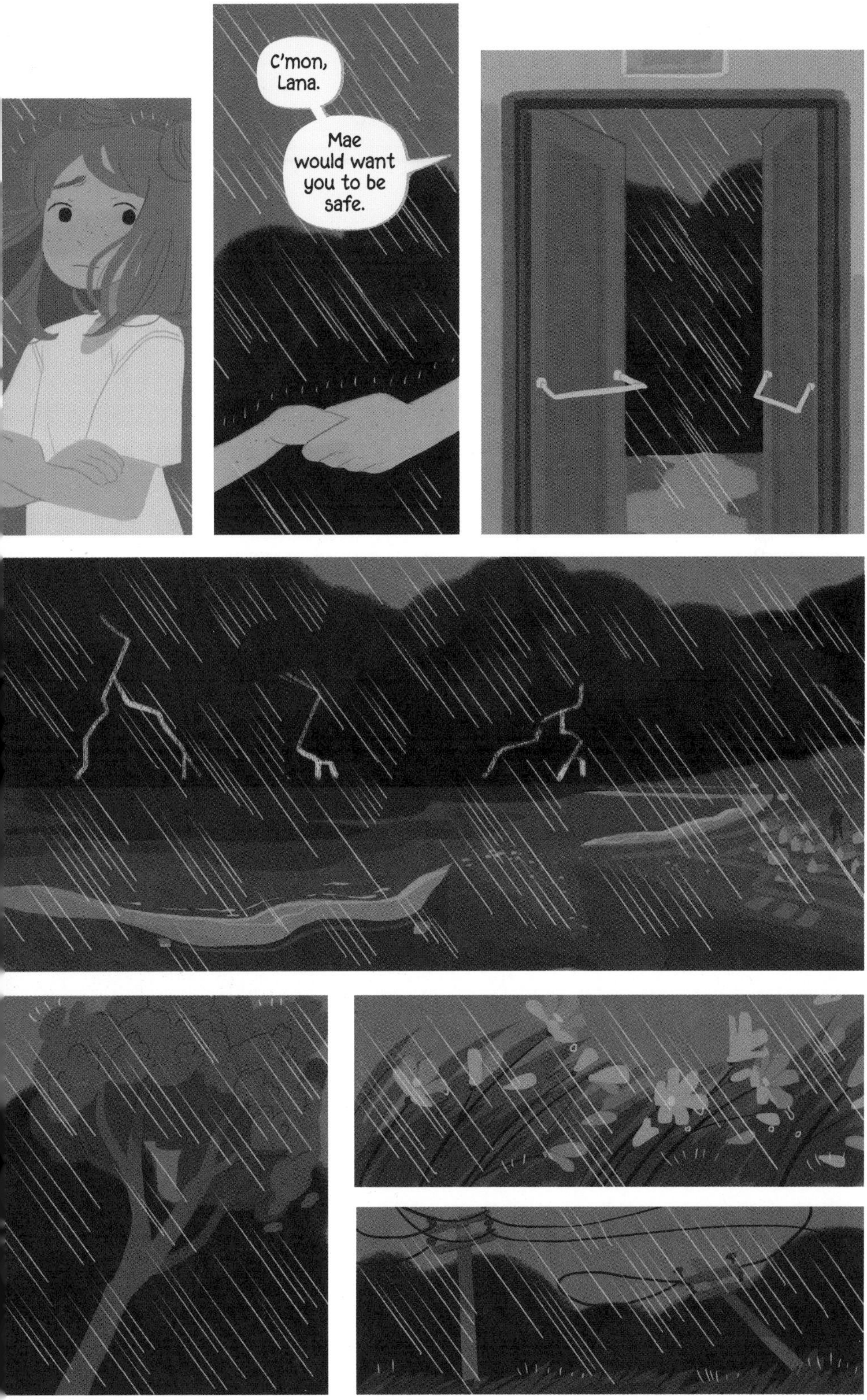
C'mon, Lana.
Mae would want you to be safe.

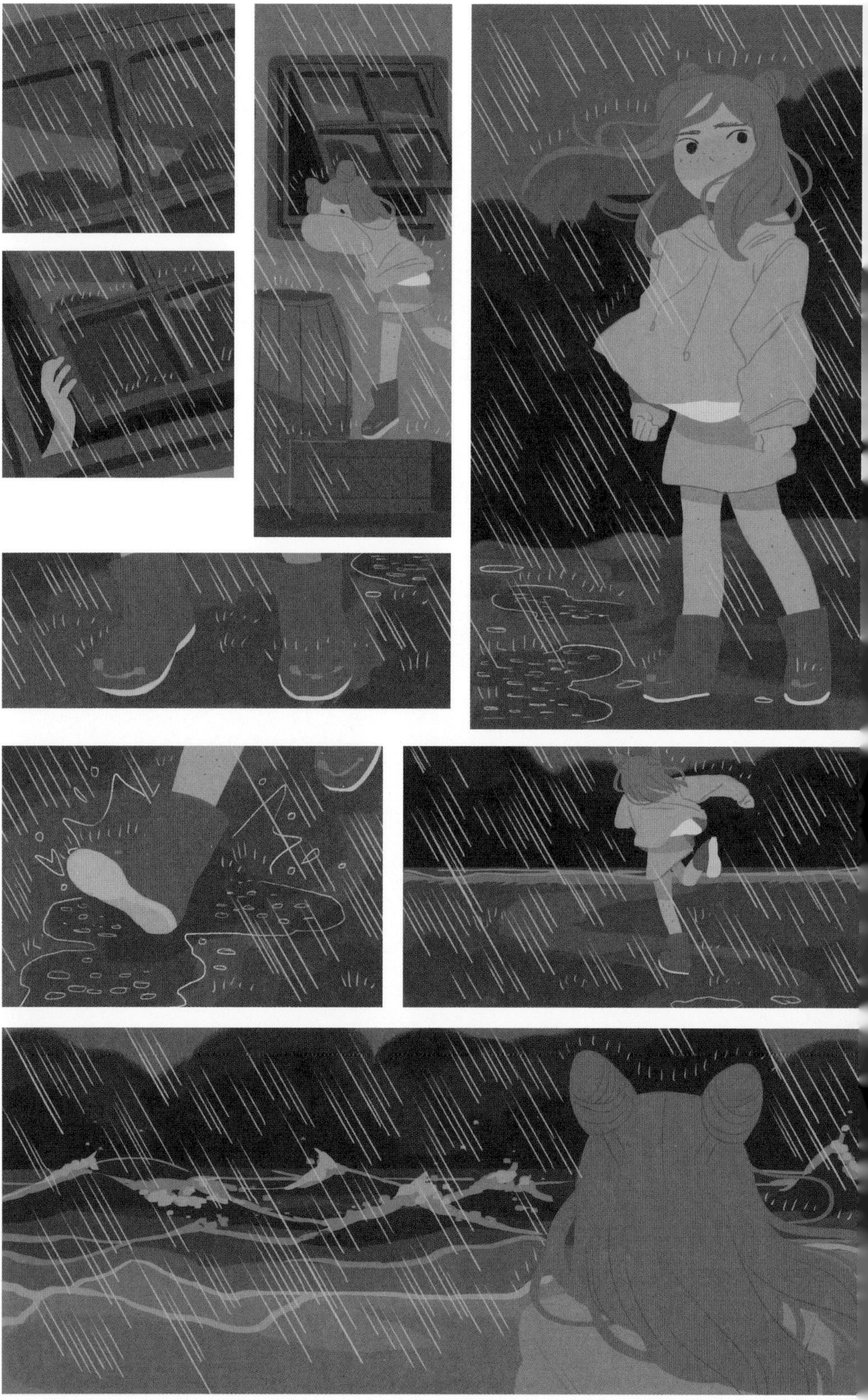

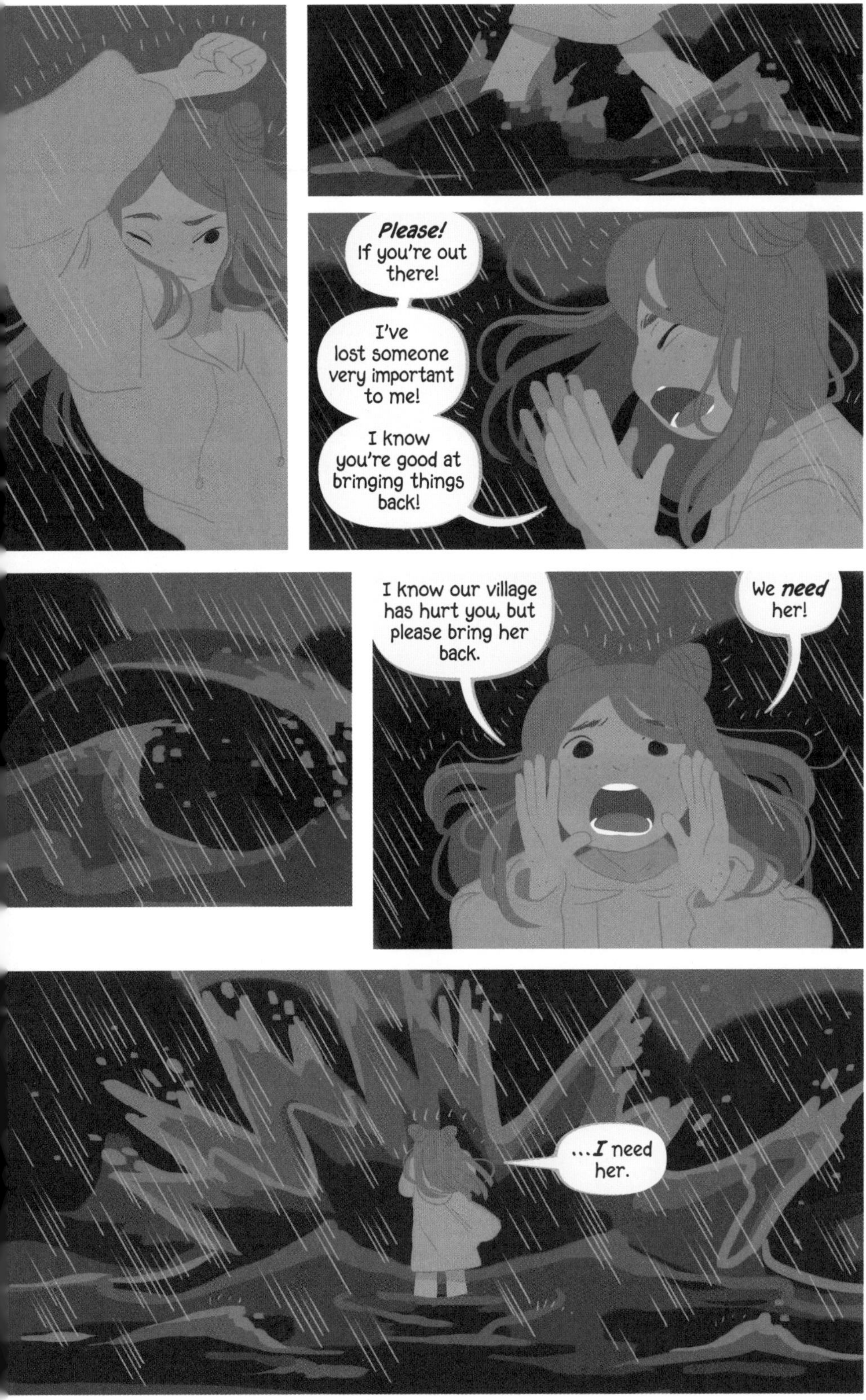
*Please!* If you're out there!
I've lost someone very important to me!
I know you're good at bringing things back!
I know our village has hurt you, but please bring her back.
We *need* her!
...*I* need her.

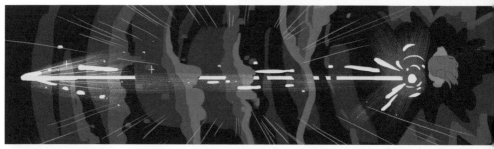

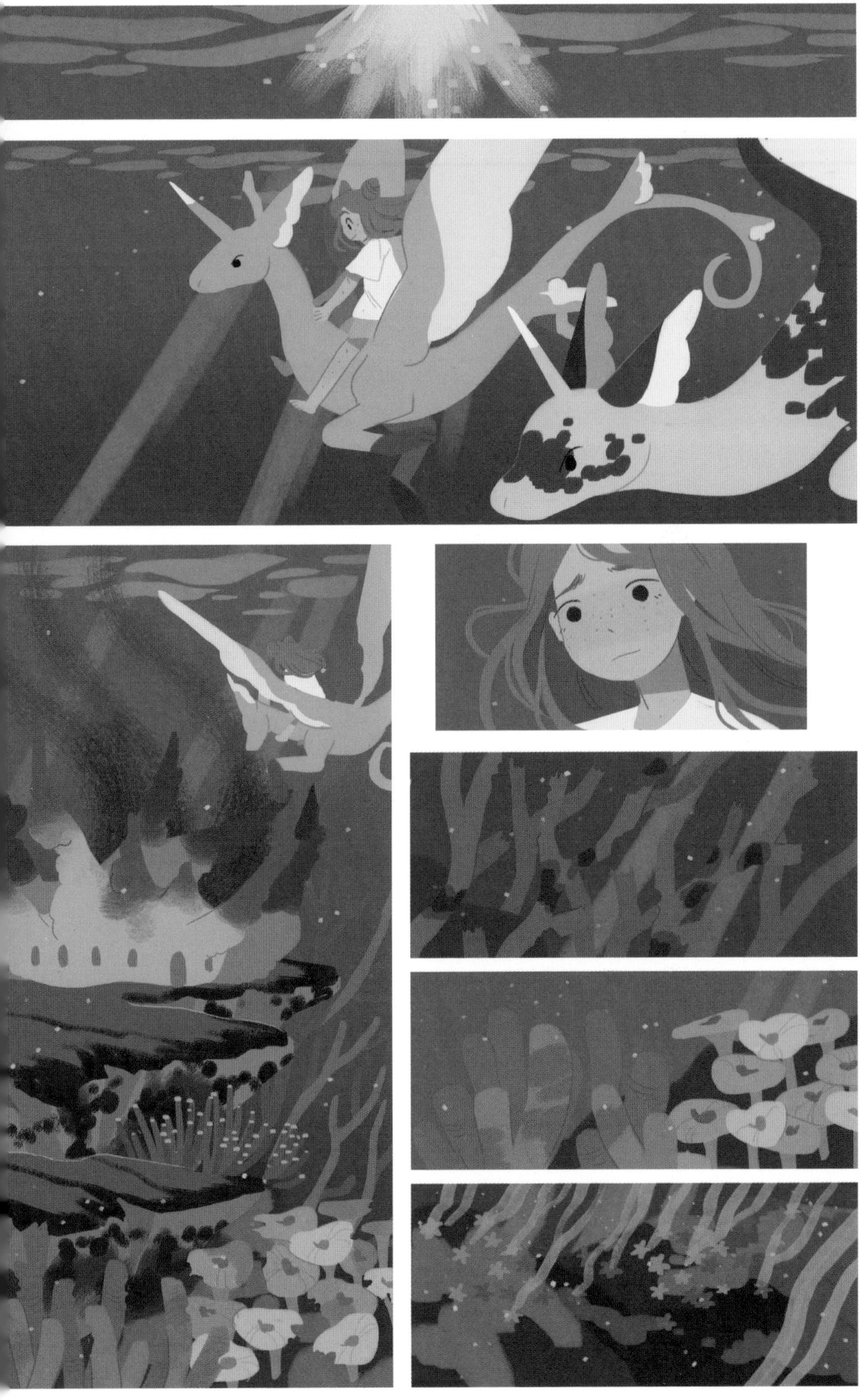

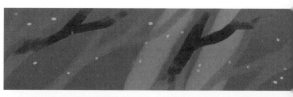

Lana!

Melody's daughter.

How did you know?

I've heard all about you and your mother.

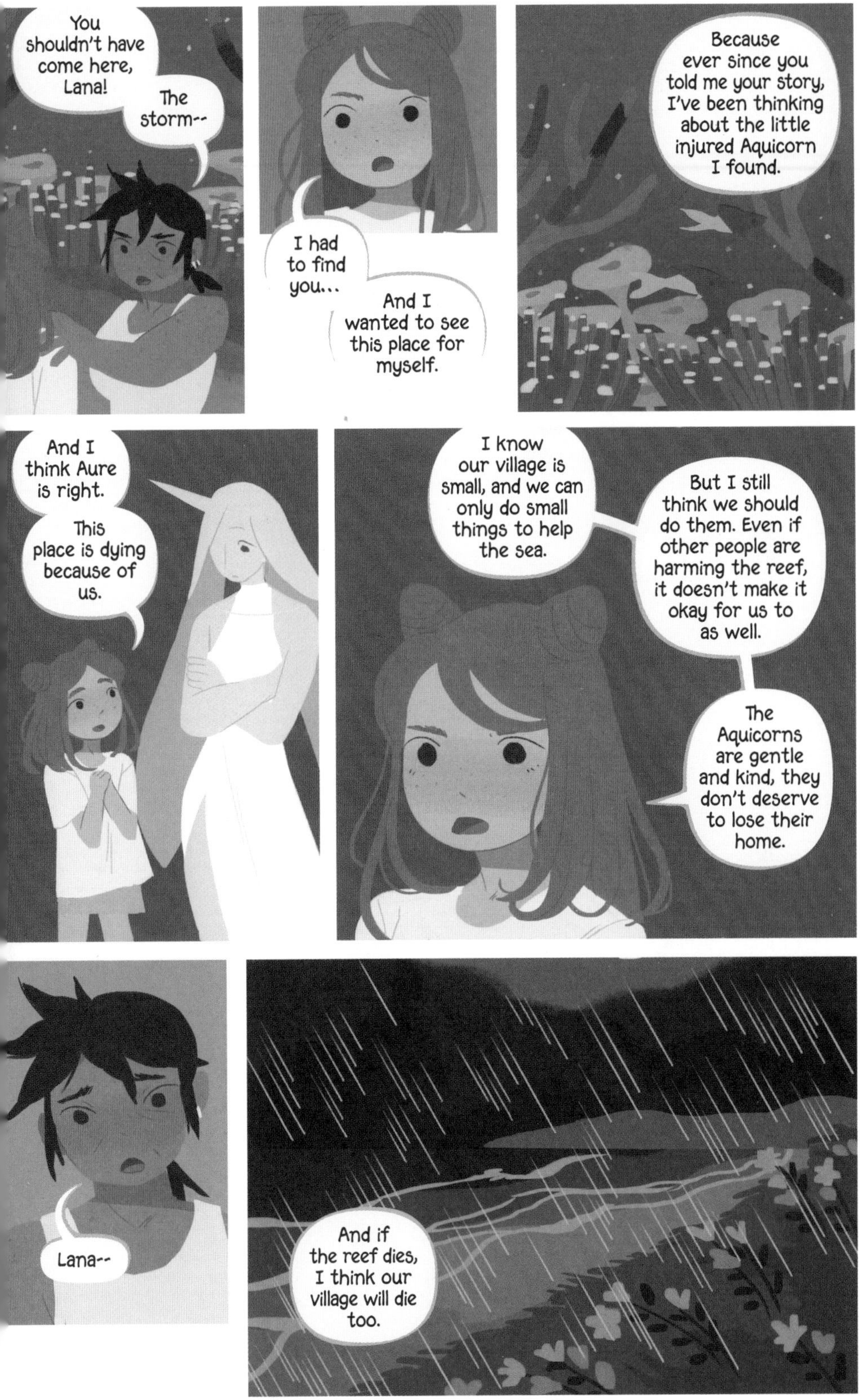
You shouldn't have come here, Lana!
The storm--
I had to find you...
And I wanted to see this place for myself.
Because ever since you told me your story, I've been thinking about the little injured Aquicorn I found.
And I think Aure is right.
This place is dying because of us.
I know our village is small, and we can only do small things to help the sea.
But I still think we should do them. Even if other people are harming the reef, it doesn't make it okay for us to as well.
The Aquicorns are gentle and kind, they don't deserve to lose their home.
Lana--
And if the reef dies, I think our village will die too.

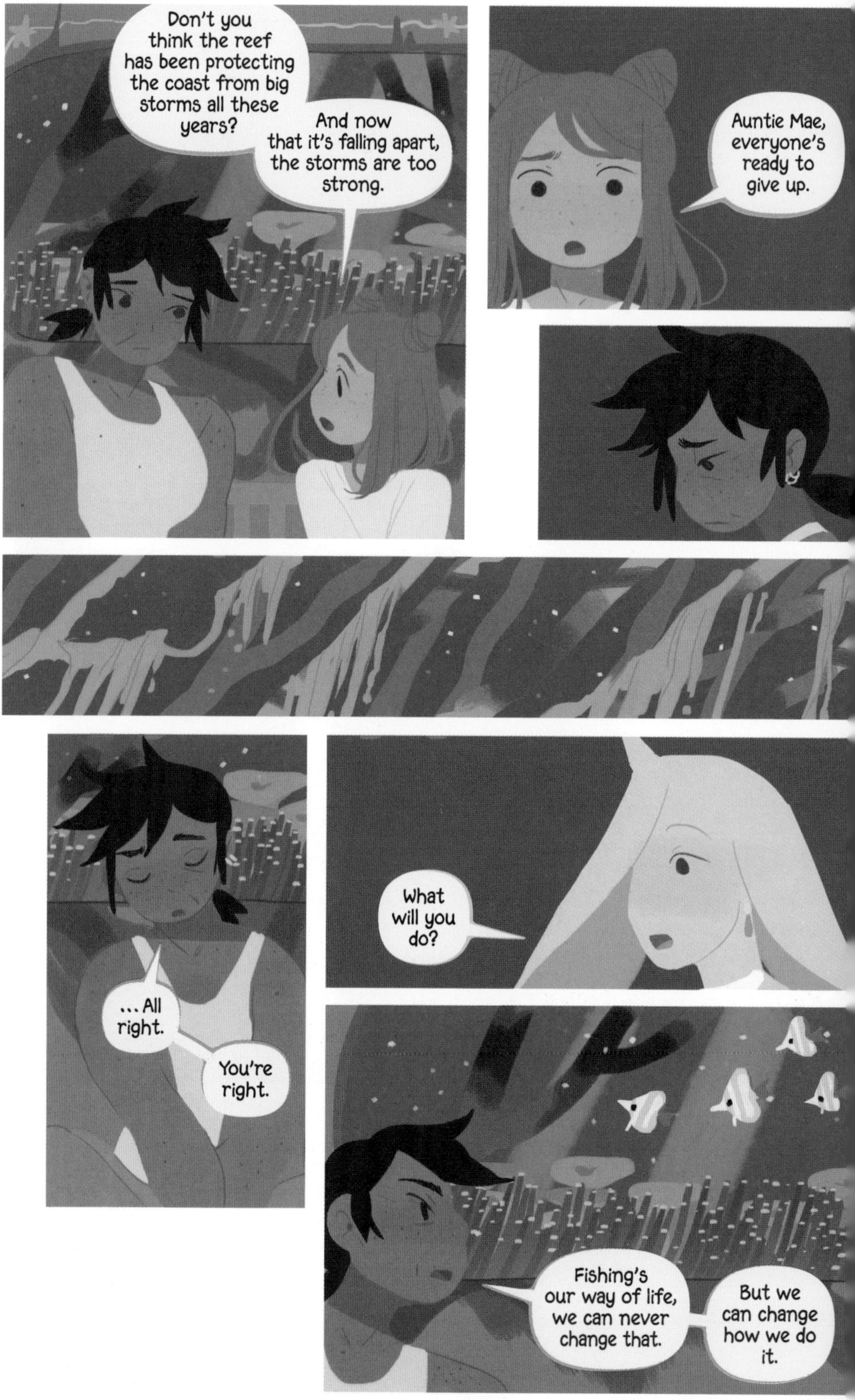
Don't you think the reef has been protecting the coast from big storms all these years?
And now that it's falling apart, the storms are too strong.
Auntie Mae, everyone's ready to give up.
...All right.
You're right.
What will you do?
Fishing's our way of life, we can never change that.
But we can change how we do it.

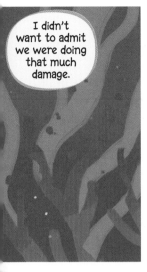

I didn't want to admit we were doing that much damage.

I wanted everyone in the village to have a good life.

To have a good, safe home.

But there's no home without a future.

I'm responsible for this.

If there's anything I can do to help it heal, I will.

There are ways, as long as the plastic nets stop.

And I'm sure we can find extra things from our cove for you to sell.

It's a deal.

Thank you, Mae.

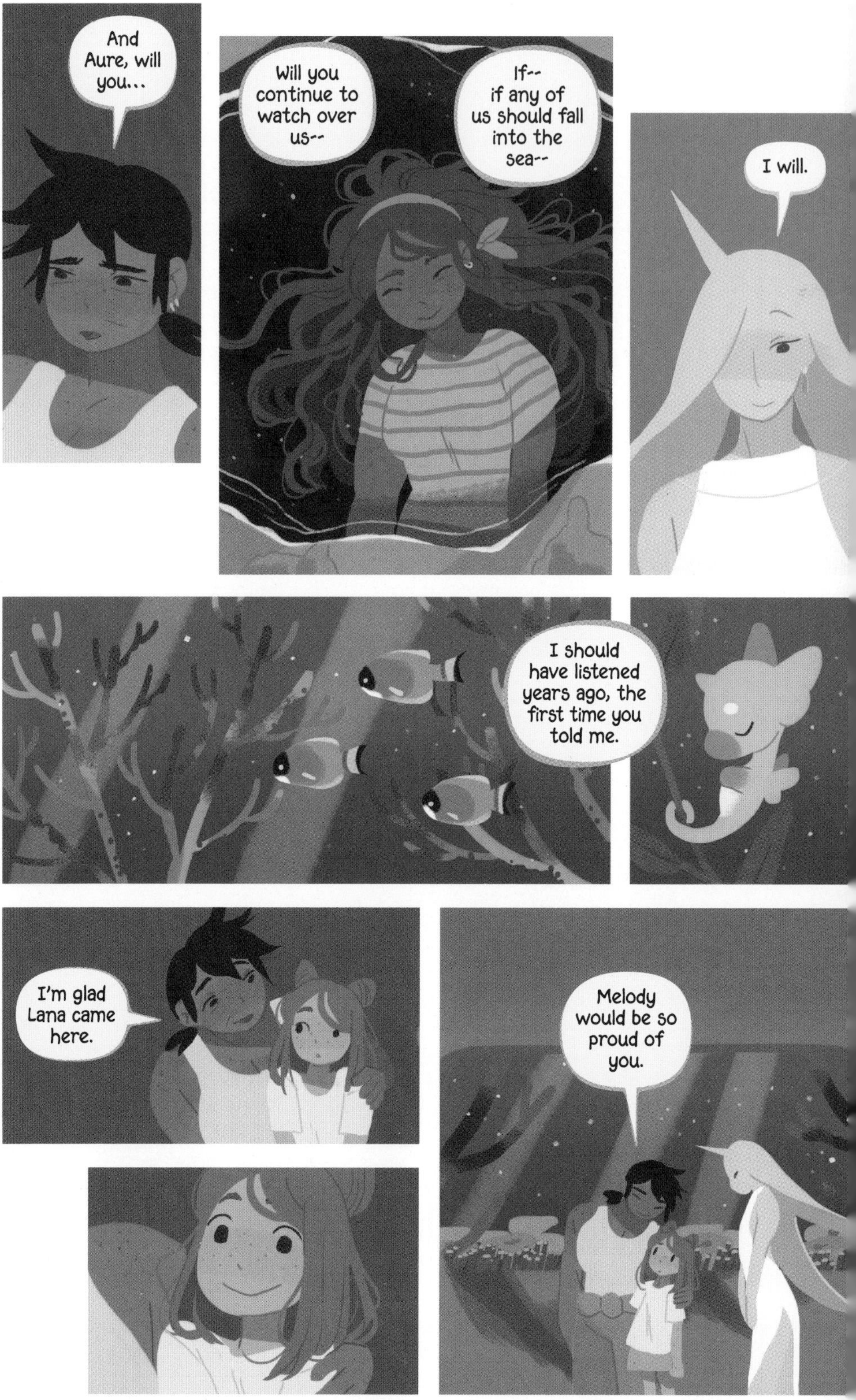
And Aure, will you...
Will you continue to watch over us--
If-- if any of us should fall into the sea--
I will.
I should have listened years ago, the first time you told me.
I'm glad Lana came here.
Melody would be so proud of you.

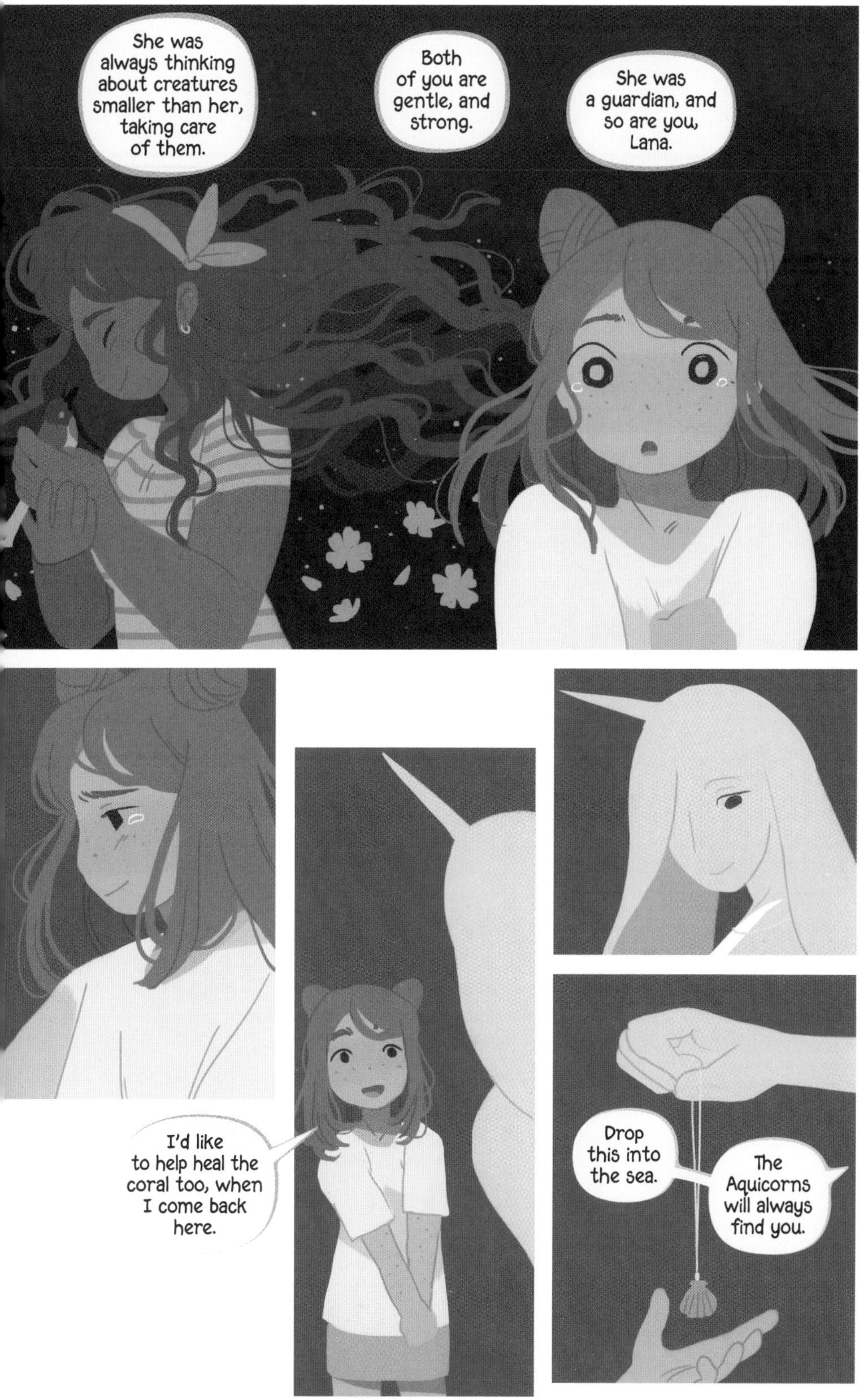
She was always thinking about creatures smaller than her, taking care of them.
Both of you are gentle, and strong.
She was a guardian, and so are you, Lana.
I'd like to help heal the coral too, when I come back here.
Drop this into the sea.
The Aquicorns will always find you.

That's the truth!

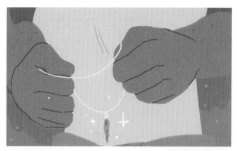

If I hadn't had this on me after Lana found it again, I think I'd have been lost to the storm.

Some things are meant to come back to you.

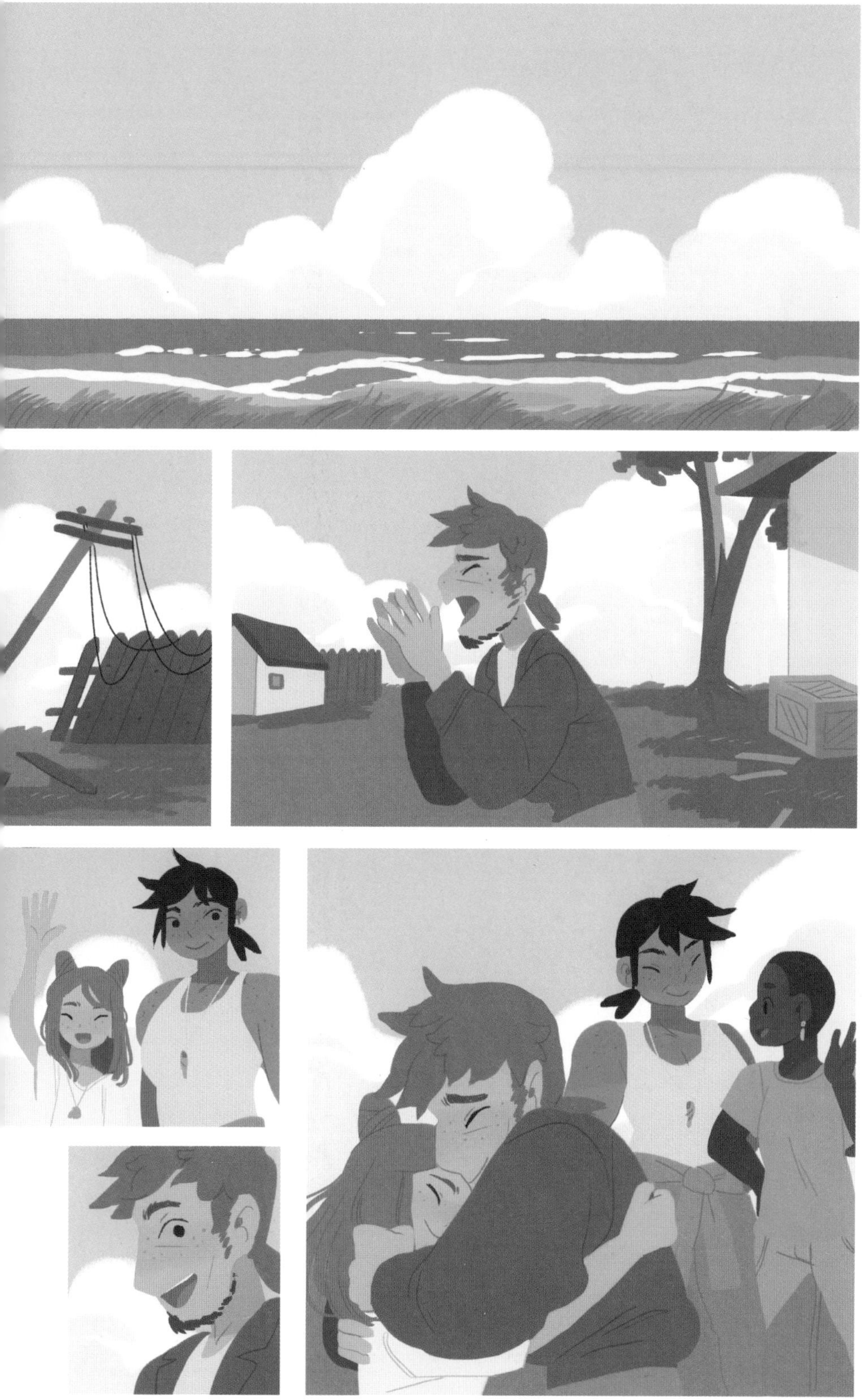

*Huh,* thought it'd look a lot worse here.

Worse? Everything's a complete mess, it's even worse than when we started cleaning up.

It's still standing, isn't it? We'll just clear it up again.

Why bother?

Another storm is just going to come and wreck it all over again.

Storms have always come, that's just nature's way. The difference is we lost our protection.

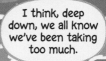

The reef sheltered our village, and now it's dying.

I think, deep down, we all know we've been taking too much.

That it wasn't right, and it couldn't last.

It's not too late--if we protect the reef, we'll survive too.

We were in balance once, we need to return to that.

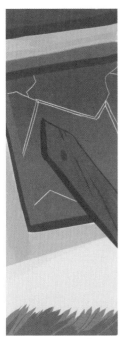

Let's get some shovels.

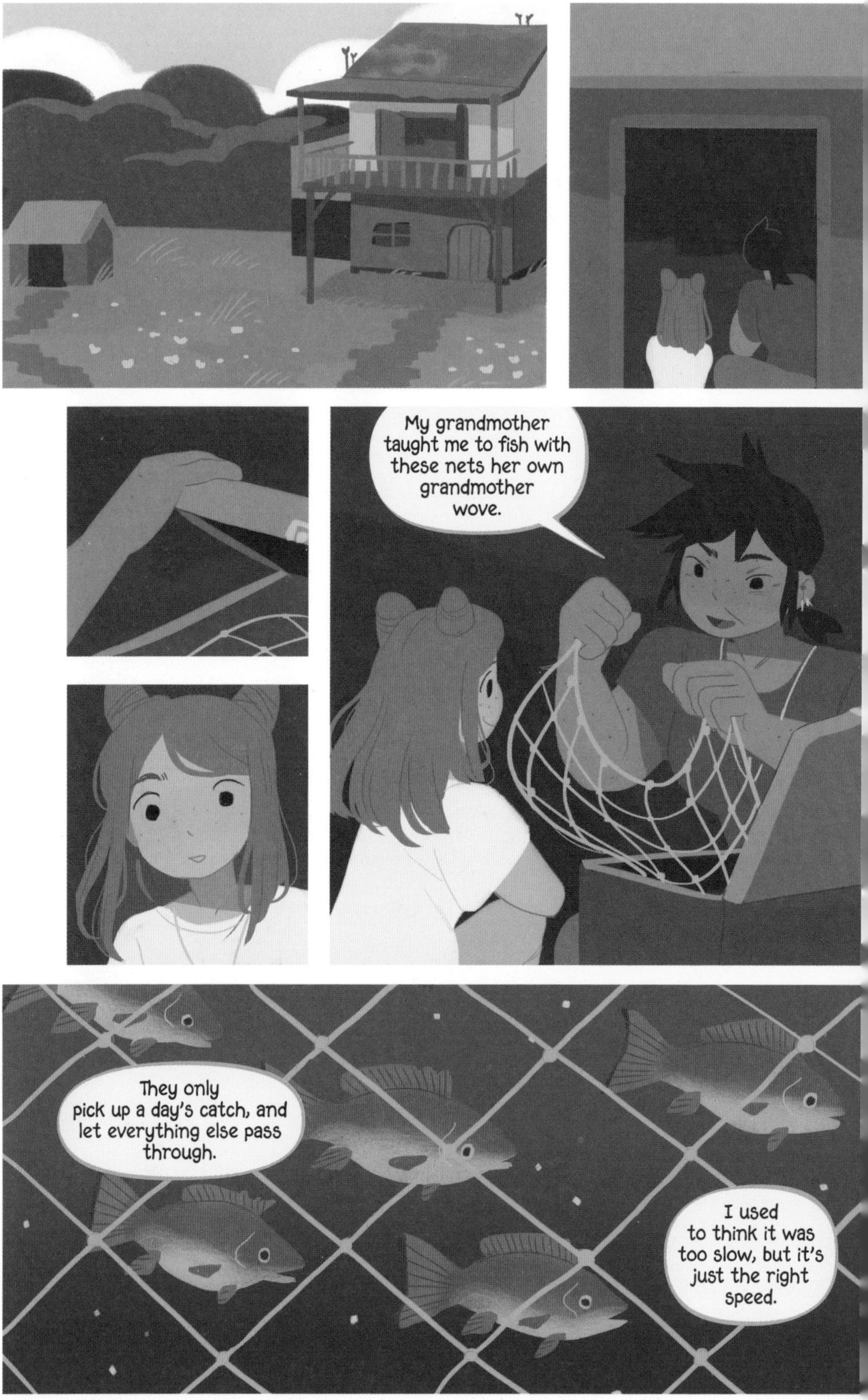
My grandmother taught me to fish with these nets her own grandmother wove.
They only pick up a day's catch, and let everything else pass through.
I used to think it was too slow, but it's just the right speed.

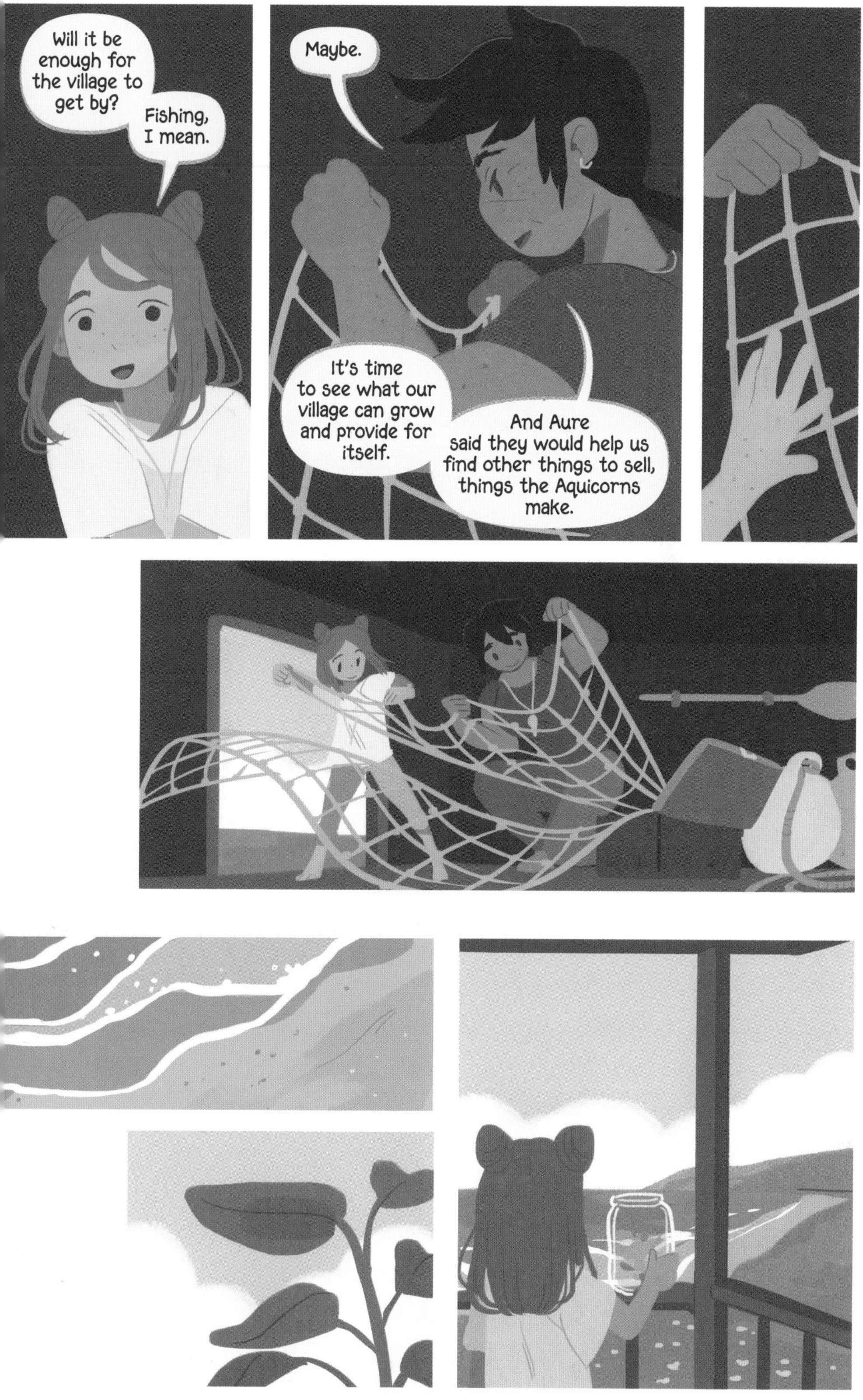
Will it be enough for the village to get by?
Fishing, I mean.
Maybe.
It's time to see what our village can grow and provide for itself.
And Aure said they would help us find other things to sell, things the Aquicorns make.

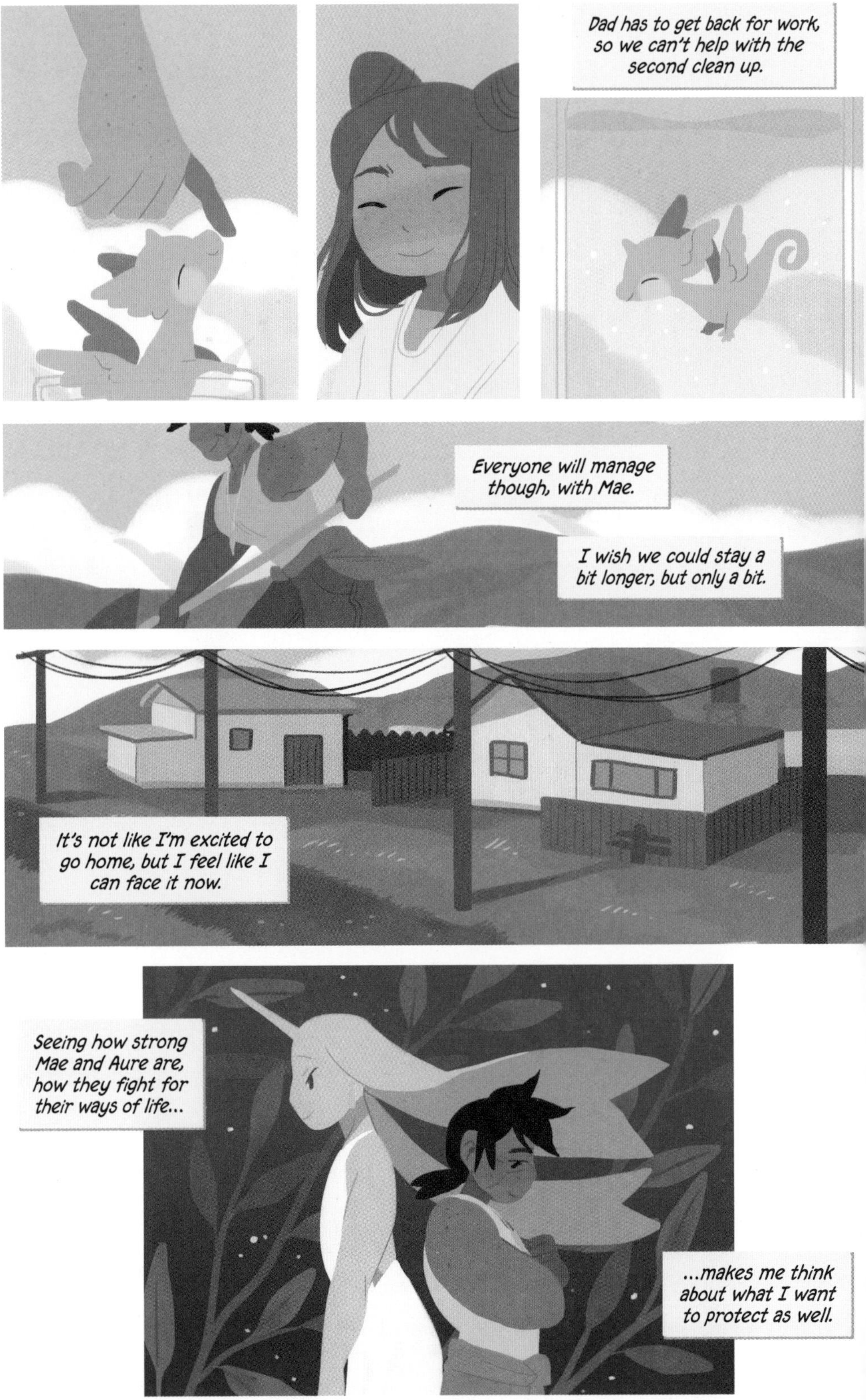
Dad has to get back for work, so we can't help with the second clean up.
Everyone will manage though, with Mae.
I wish we could stay a bit longer, but only a bit.
It's not like I'm excited to go home, but I feel like I can face it now.
Seeing how strong Mae and Aure are, how they fight for their ways of life...
...makes me think about what I want to protect as well.

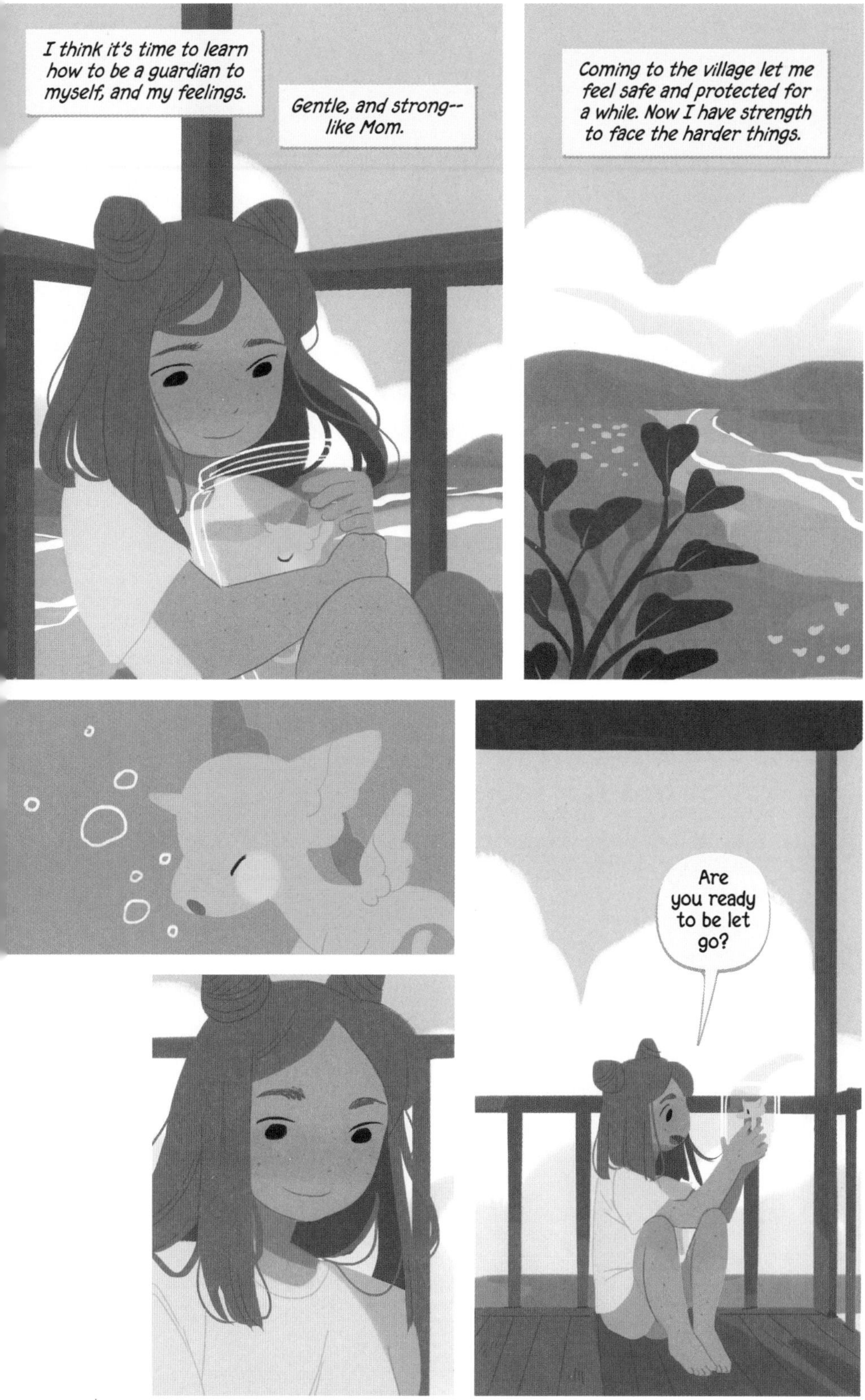
I think it's time to learn how to be a guardian to myself, and my feelings.
Gentle, and strong-- like Mom.
Coming to the village let me feel safe and protected for a while. Now I have strength to face the harder things.
Are you ready to be let go?

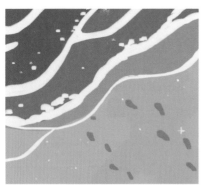

You'll do fine!

Thank you for taking care of this little one, Lana.

You are welcome to visit us anytime.

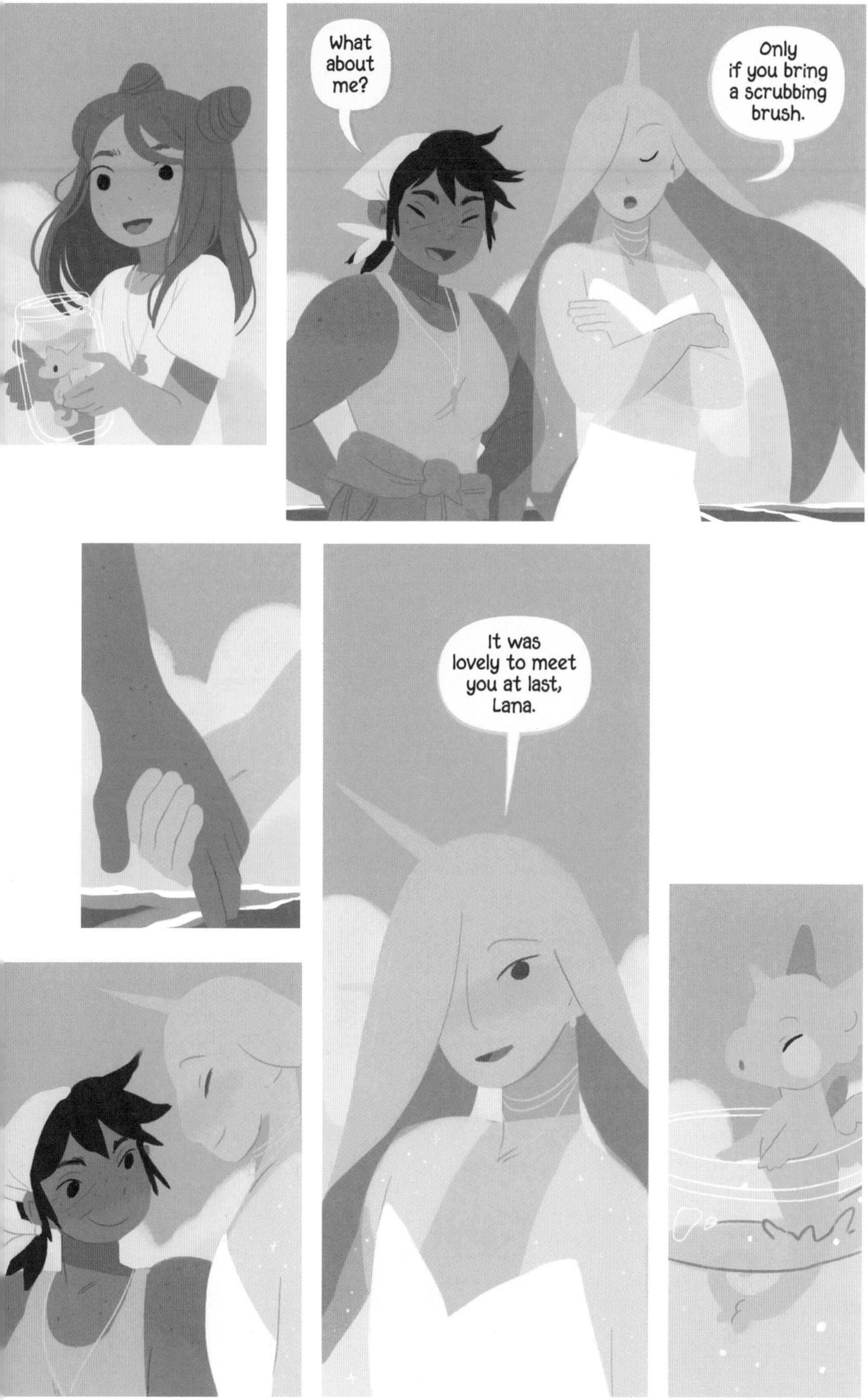
What about me?
Only if you bring a scrubbing brush.
It was lovely to meet you at last, Lana.

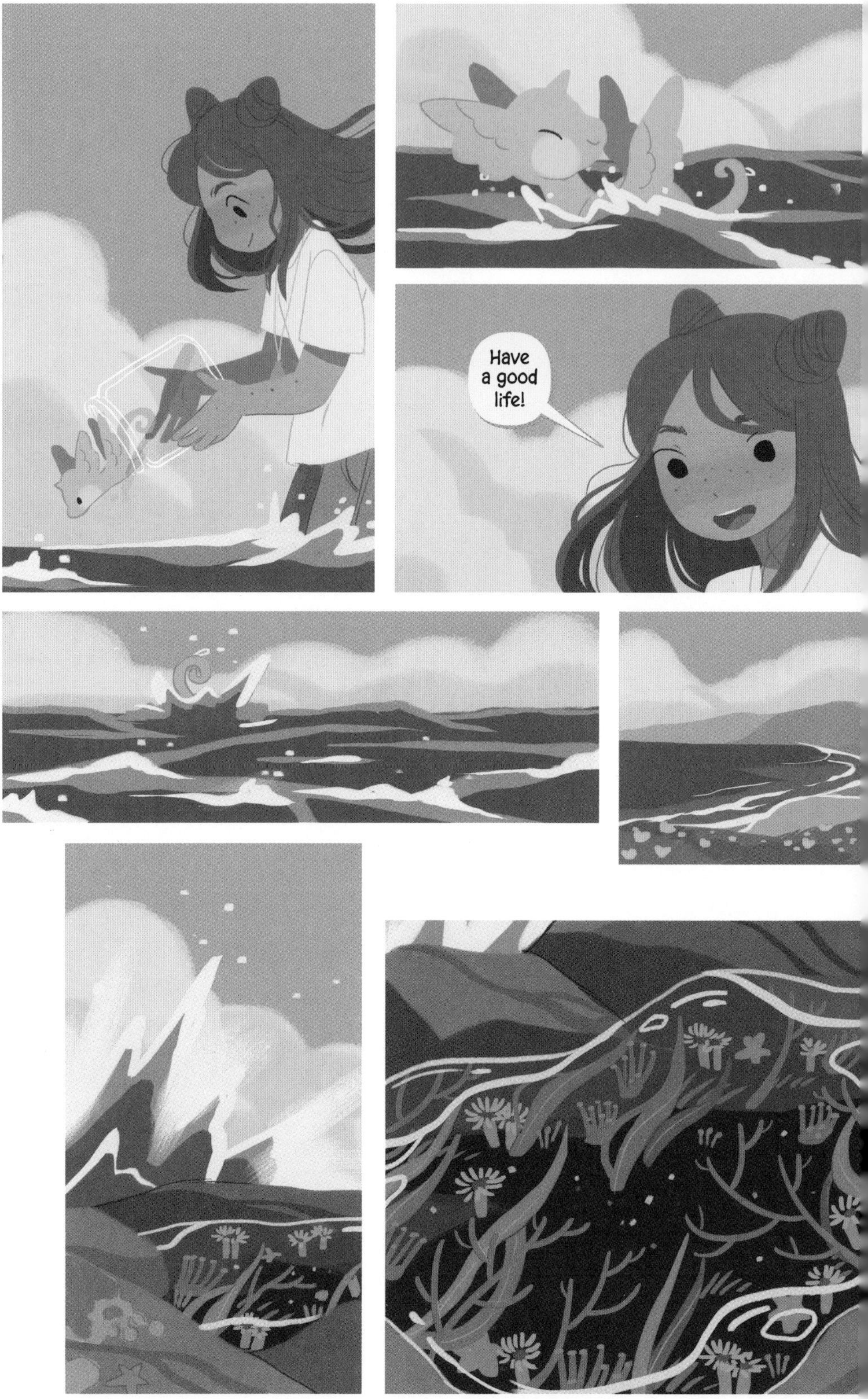
Have a good life!

The End

## WHAT ARE CORAL REEFS?

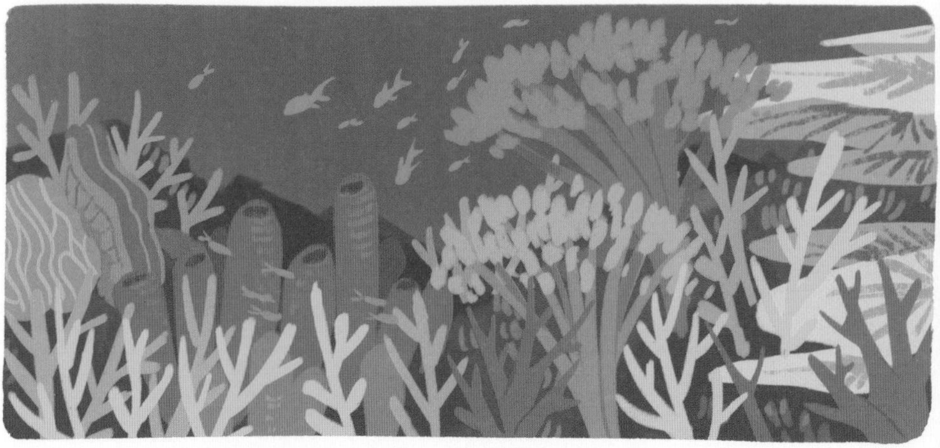

Coral reefs are actually built by living creatures—the corals themselves! These tiny creatures create calcium carbonate, which hardens and becomes a platform for the many different types of corals to live on, as well as sea anemones and seaweed. They are extremely diverse environments, which means they're home to thousands of different species of fish, worms, crustaceans, sponges, and other creatures, all of which can't live anywhere else. All these different creatures live in balance with one another, sometimes helping each other to survive by offering protection or food. If one of these species were to become sick or unhealthy (just as the Aquicorns do in the story), it can affect many other species as well. Compared to the size of the ocean, coral reefs are quite small and scattered throughout the globe, so it's important for us to protect these unique sanctuaries.

## WHERE CAN YOU FIND CORAL REEFS?

Coral reefs prefer shallow, warm water close to the surface. (However, there are some deeper, cold water corals as well!) This means they usually live in tropical waters, mostly around the equator. Here the water is just the right temperature for them to thrive. Most of the coral reefs in the world are found in the Indo-Pacific region, which includes the Indian Ocean, the Pacific Ocean, and the seas in between.

The largest and most famous coral reef is the Great Barrier Reef, which lies off the coast of Australia. You'll also find large reefs off the coast of Mexico and Florida, as well as around many Pacific and Southeast Asian islands.

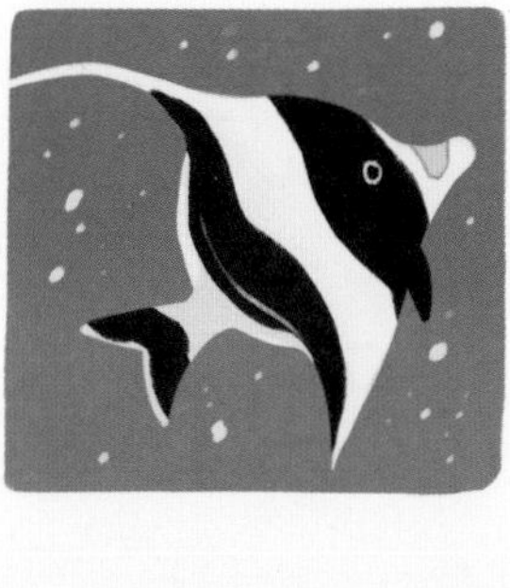

## WHAT IS CAUSING DAMAGE TO CORAL REEFS?

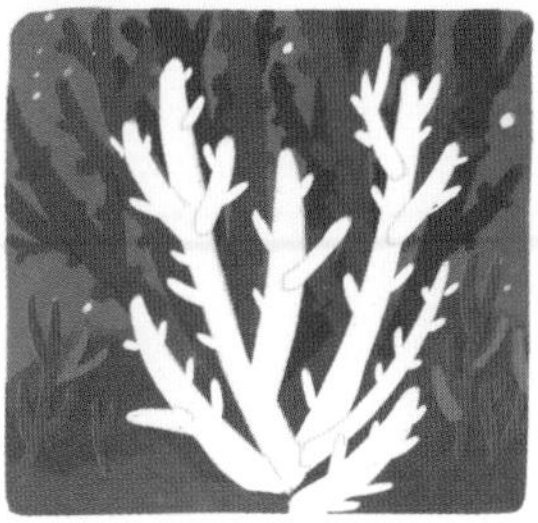

For a long time, humans either didn't know or didn't care whether the ways we treat the ocean might harm coral reefs. Thankfully, we can now test and keep track of the coral health, and see how our human activities have affected the reef. Now that we know, it's our responsibility to protect them in any way we can.

The issues that hurt coral reefs most are by-products of much larger problems, such as the ocean warming through climate change, large-scale pollution, and overfishing. Fishing gear can damage the reef directly by crashing into it, breaking the coral and damaging it beyond its ability to recover. Pollution from the land, caused by either natural run-off (liquids naturally moving towards the sea), or through dumping, puts chemicals into the water that can hurt and eventually kill the delicate coral. Rising temperatures of the sea cause "coral bleaching," which kills an essential algae that lives in the coral, and in turn the coral may die too.

## HOW CAN WE STOP THIS DAMAGE?

As individuals, it can feel difficult to stand up to huge, global problems such as overfishing, climate change, and pollution. This is why it's important to form communities, and to gather as many voices as we can to make ourselves heard. We can tell politicians and businesses that any methods that harm the sea need to change. Raising awareness and telling other people why we need to protect our oceans is the way to build a tide that can eventually turn things around. For problems on this scale, public knowledge is the key.

On a personal level, consider what plastic or chemicals you might be putting into the environment in your day-to-day life. Consider supporting brands and businesses that are aware of climate issues, and avoid those that choose to ignore the problem. Let local politicians know that the environment is important to you, and will affect who you support.

Thankfully, there are groups throughout the globe that are monitoring, researching, and trying to find ways to protect our reefs. Many of these are charitable organizations, so offering a donation is a great way to support direct action towards marine preservation. It's also important to make sure that local communities are still able to make a living with these changes. Finding new ways to create income, such as tourism or alternative methods of fishing, is vital.

It is possible to grow and "farm" corals, which can be then reattached to the reef. It is also possible to create the ocean layer on which the corals grow, and growing in captivity increases the success and growth rates of the coral. This is hopeful, but we need to make sure that these corals have a safe and healthy sea to live in once they are transplanted back into the ocean.

Now is the time for us to be guardians to the sea, in return for the life it has given our planet.

FOR MORE INFORMATION

**CORAL REEF CONSERVATION ALLIANCE (WWW.CORAL.ORG)** — CORAL is a great place to learn more about coral reefs throughout the world, about how organisations are working to protect them, and how you can help be a guardian of the reef too.

**UN ENVIRONMENT (WWW.UNENVIRONMENT.ORG)** — If you're interested in other conservation issues and ways to protect the planet, the UN Environment is an excellent starting point. They cover a range of topics, as well as new technology designed to help the environment.

Ask your local librarian for book recommendations!

Katie O'Neill is an illustrator and graphic novelist from New Zealand, and author of *Princess Princess Ever After*, *The Tea Dragon Society*, and *Aquicorn Cove*, all from Oni Press. She makes gentle fantasy stories for younger readers, and is very interested in tea, creatures, things that grow, and the magic of everyday life.

## Look for Katie's next book
### COMING FALL 2019!

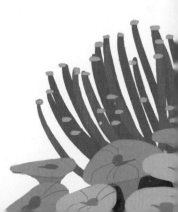

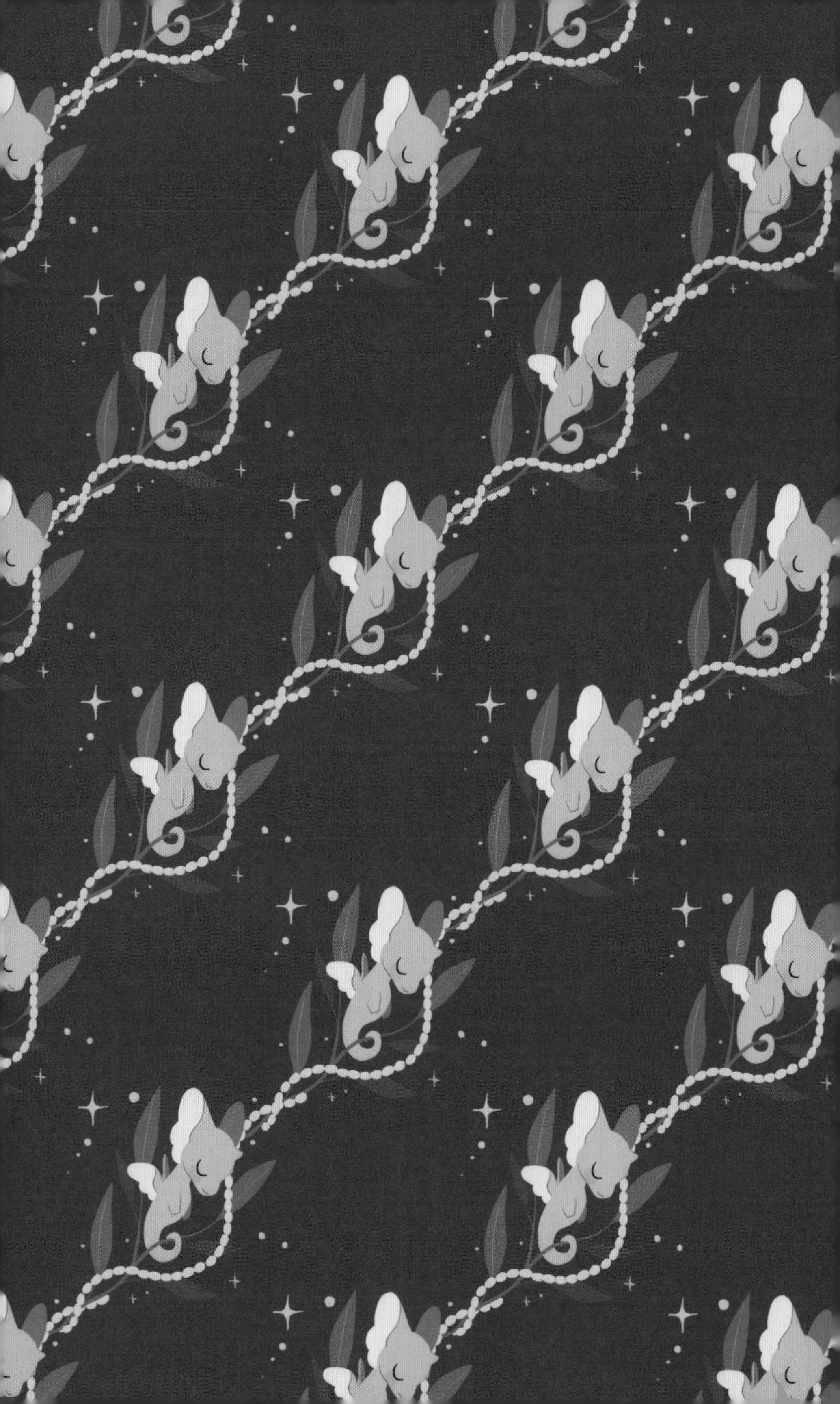

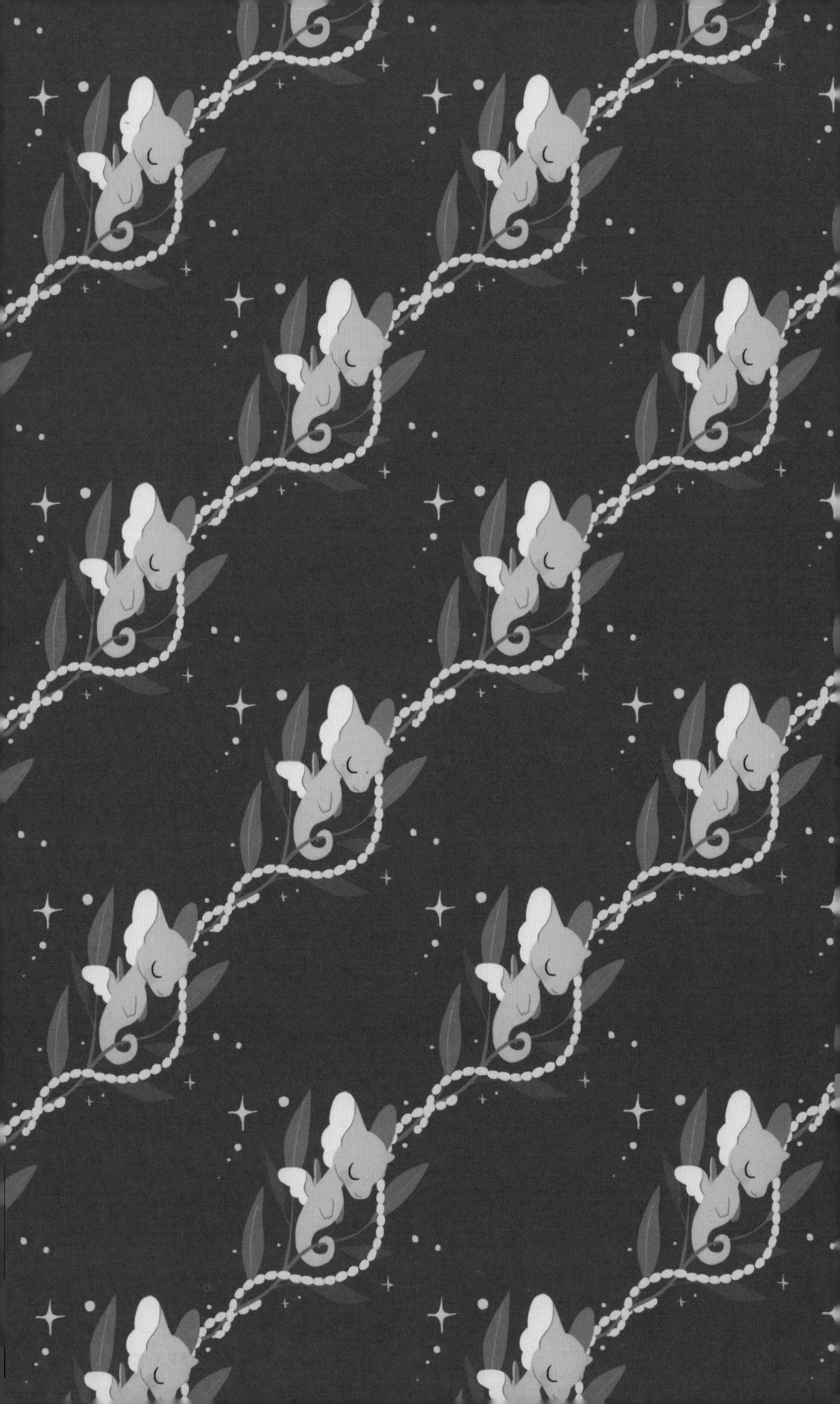